T0304468

Other Works by the Author:

Novels:

Oldcat & Ms. Puss: A Book of Days for You and Me

Let There Be Lite: OR, How I Came To Know and Love Godel's Incompleteness Theorem

Pineapple: A Comic Novel in Verse

The Theoretics of Love

Back to the Wine Jug: A Comic Novel in Verse

Story Collections:

Some Heroes, Some Heroines, Some Others

The World's Thinnest Fat Man

Masques for the Fields of Time

Ghostly Demarcations

Edited by:

Belles Letters: Contemporary Fiction by Alabama Women

Tartts 1-7: Incisive Fiction by new Writers

The Alleged Woman

A True Tale of Ballot Intrigue

Joe Taylor

Livingston Press

The University of West Alabama

ISBN 13: trade paper 978-1-60489-284-0
ISBN 13: e-book 978-1-60489-285-7

Library of Congress Control Number: 2021930097
Printed on acid-free paper
Printed in the United States of America by
Publishers Graphics

Typesetting and page layout: Joe Taylor
Proofreading: Christin Loehr, Tricia Taylor
Cover Design: Joe Taylor
Front Cover Photo: Amanda Nolin
Back Cover Photo: Tricia Taylor

For The Sumter Scribblers, Christin Loehr, Sarah Langcuster (in absentia, get well soon, Sarah), and Tricia Taylor. Also for Joy Cauthron, who gave the nudge needed for this novel.

This is a work of fiction. Any resemblance
to persons living or dead is coincidental.
Livingston Press is part of The University of West Alabama,
and thereby has non-profit status.
Donations are tax-deductible.

6 5 4 3 2 1

The Alleged Woman

A True Tale of Ballot Intrigue

"Anyone can count: 1, 2, 3, 5 . . . anyone can add: 2 + 2 = 8. Remember, Rudy, it's the higher maths and geometries that befuddle most people. Go for those. And take an apple with you."

—Sir Isaac Newton, in a night-vision preparing Rudy Giuliani for his appearance before Georgia officials to demand a third ballot recount.

Breaking News! *FBI Finds Nearly Seven Million Biden Ballots in Alabama Woman's Car!* Sumter County, Alabama: Upon responding to a routine mid-morning request to repair a flat tire, Alabama FBI agents found the trunk of a Sumter County woman's black Nissan Altima filled with ballots listing Joe Biden for President. Agents also found eleven books of first-class Elvis stamps in the Altima's glove compartment. "We speculate she was planning on mailing these to the local voting station. Had she been able to do so, all of Alabama's electoral votes would have gone to the Biden campaign. We can just thank alert agents who acted quickly on finding the nearly seven million ballots," a federal law enforcement official who wished to remain anonymous commented.

Update! *Alleged Woman!* The alleged woman who, according to a local poll supervisor, had over seven million Biden ballots in the trunk of her car is now being held on Suspicion. The alleged woman whose black Nissan Altima contained well over seven million illegal Presidential ballots for Joe Biden and ten books of first-class stamps is now being held in Sumter County Jail on a charge of Suspicion.

***Breaking News*!** *FBI Questions Poll Supervisor's Numbers!* Southwest Alabama Field Agent Sam Strong questioned the numbers released by Poll Supervisor Eve Adams yesterday. "We counted eleven booklets of stamps. And just a bit under seven million ballots. I want to keep the exact number under wraps for security reasons. And I hereby emphasize that the first thing all agents go through is a month-long course in counting. This course, The Hoover Number Assessment Protocol, was instigated by Mr. J. Edgar Hoover himself, and it involves instant amount appraisal and employs memory devices for numbers, be they Arab, Roman, or otherwise." When asked if the memory devices might involve fingers and toes, Field Agent Strong replied that the methodology was classified information. "You do know that Sumter County is among the poorest in the nation, so a single one of those stamp booklets would make a very attractive catch," he added. When then asked why the polling agents might exaggerate the ballot count, Agent Strong answered, "Those folk down there are attention-hungry. They think any attention will land them jobs and money. Maybe a new needle manufacturing plant. Maybe a new plastic garbage can manufacturer. I don't know, maybe a way to recycle cat litter. Jobs, jobs, jobs. That's all they're interested in. I need to add here that my supervisors in Birmingham and Atlanta and even Washington are considering an FBI recount of both those stamp booklets and those ballots."

In related news, the alleged woman, whose name is still being withheld pending notification of some people, broke her silence and admitted, "I used one of those stamps to pay the gas bill. Please tell Joe I'm sorry." When asked if she meant the alleged President-elect, the woman refused to answer. When asked how many booklets were in her glove compartment, the alleged woman said, "I've never been good at numbers." The alleged woman's bail has been set at $143. It's uncertain whether she will meet that bail.

In news elsewhere, the governor of Alabama has fired Alabama's Secretary of Defense. Livingston Mayor Babette "Babes" Babcock could not be reached for comment, but Poll Supervisor Eve Adams said, "This is very troubling. Sumter County's eastern (sic) boundary borders on Lauderdale County and Meridian, Mississippi. Those folk have always been jealous of our resources. I just don't know what might happen without a good Secretary of Defense."

Update! *Ballot Count Confirmed!* Sumter County voting supervisor Eve Adams has confirmed that over seven million ballots were found in a black Nissan Altima. "Soon as we saw that hunk of ballots the FBI dropped off, we knew there was more than seven million," Ms. Adams stated. "Our first count came to seven million and one.

With a number that large, you just got to count twice, so we did and come up with seven million and three. Frankly, my four poll volunteers are as old as them candidates up there in Washington, so I got some young blood in and they confirmed seven million and two, two separate times. I'm confident of that number. A number of fake ballots like that would have been a slap in the face to Sumter County and to all of Alabama."

When asked about the eleven books of stamps found in the Nissan's glove compartment, Ms. Adams replied, "I don't know where the FBI got that eleven number. We counted only ten."

When asked about the alleged relationship between the alleged woman who had the alleged ballots in her Nissan's alleged trunk and her alleged mother who worked at the alleged Livingston post office, Ms. Adams replied, "I feel heavy tulips for her. I'm a mother myself. I got two children in grade school and one starting high. You just hate to see one of your own in trouble. Listen here, I don't got time for fiddle-faddle questions. I need to get to work." Ms. Adams reportedly held her palm in a young, polite reporter's face to end the interview.

In related news, the Nissan owner's identity is still being withheld pending notification of some people. She is being held under Suspicion, and her bail has not been set, despite a prior report. The FBI is investigating the alleged mother of the alleged woman, who allegedly recently retired from the local post office in Livingston. Not the alleged woman, just to clarify, but the alleged woman's alleged mother—she allegedly retired from the Livingston post office.

Update! *Woman Out on Bond!* The alleged woman whose black Nissan allegedly held counterfeit ballots is out on bond after a Sumter County judge finalized the bail amount and another woman posted her $134 bond. (A previous report had mistakenly set the bail at $143.) "I don't even know this alleged woman. At least I don't think I do. I may have seen her in the produce aisle testing a cantaloupe or watermelon for ripeness. I'm just a concerned citizen," Patty "Pearl" Pureheart commented after posting the bond. The alleged woman, whose name is still being withheld pending notification of some people, at first refused to leave the county jail, balking at a requirement that she wear an ankle monitor. "Ankle bracelets are what loose women wear! If God had meant humans to wear ankle bracelets," she continued. The remainder of her comment was cut off by a freight train passing the jail. The alleged woman finally did accept a facemask with a radio implant. Sumter County's sheriff, Brandon "Big" Biggs, commented, "We just don't want someone desperate like this clomping off to Cuba, Canada, California, or some other communist country. If she wants to wear a mask instead of an ankle bracelet, well, that's fine by me. I don't know what she means by 'loose women.' My daughter goes to church regular-like and she wanted a ruby ankle bracelet for her sixteenth birthday. Wears it, too, after me and her mother bought her a nice one with three tiny, polite rubies."

In related news, the FBI is reportedly moving closer to insisting on a recount of the stamp booklets found in the alleged woman's glove compartment, plus the ballots found in her alleged trunk. "We just have trouble with those numbers the Sumter polling office gave us," FBI agent Sam Strong reported. The agent also noted that the alleged woman's mother, who recently retired from the local post office, may be under investigation. Agent Strong did not specify any reason for this second investigation.

In news elsewhere, Alabama's governor has yet to name a new Secretary of Defense.

Up to the Minute News! *FBI to Recount!* Agent Sam Strong announced that he has requested field agents from Georgia to travel to Sumter County and perform a recount on the stamp booklets and the "Ballistic Biden Ballots," as they have come to be called locally. "I requested agents from Georgia because of their experience in hand-counting large numbers. They will monitor the recount. Because of COVID regulations, they will have to so-called social distance at six feet. However, we will issue military grade binoculars to the six or nine agents to assure no sleight of hand occurs. I expect the agents to arrive late this afternoon. The recount will begin at dawn tomorrow."

In related news, Agent Strong announced that the mother of the alleged woman, whose name is still being withheld pending notification of some people, is now under investigation for possible alleged postal fraud. "Those eleven booklets of stamps are just too convenient," Agent Strong added. When reminded that the Sumter polling authority claimed there were only ten booklets, Agent Strong waved a dismissive hand, saying, "That number's exactly what the trained Georgia agents will investigate, isn't it?"

Update! *Mother Confesses!* The mother of the alleged woman whose Nissan Altima held either slightly over or slightly under seven million forged ballots for Joe Biden—a recount is being held—has admitted that she gave her daughter—the alleged woman—a number of books of first-class stamps. "My supervisor at the P.O. told us that a directive had come down to destroy all those Elvis stamps because they were causing sightings of his ghost across the country. That's crazy, too crazy." The woman went on to say that she "couldn't just dump Elvis in some dirty creek filled with crawlfish," so she gave them to her daughter. When asked how many booklets of stamps she gave the alleged woman, the mother indicated that she couldn't remember. Birmingham FBI is now holding a recount of the booklets. There may have been as many as fourteen according to one source who wished to remain anonymous.

In other news, the alleged woman has retired to her family's farm and is refusing contact with the press. "Just ask Joe," she said. When asked whether she meant Joe Biden or her uncle, Joe Smithers up in Winston County, she only shook her head. "I will say this," the alleged woman announced before shutting the door in this reporter's face, "I need my Nissan back. That is, unless this county wants me to go on unemployment. I don't know a thing about those things in its trunk. I had a flat tire, maybe two. For all I know, I bought the car that way. Not with the flat tire, but with the trunk full of stuff. Maybe it came that way from Japan. I don't mess with mechanical matters like trunks. I had a flat tire, maybe two, or I wouldn't even have known the car had a stupid trunk. I don't do much travelling."

Update! *Conspiracy Theories Fueled!* With yesterday's statement by the mother of the alleged woman about the first-class Elvis stamps, theories have multiplied that postal authorities in Washington, D.C., are behind the dissemination of the seventeen booklets—the exact number has yet to be confirmed by the Birmingham FBI—in an attempt to throw Alabama's electoral votes to Joe Biden, while installing a Republican ex-Auburn football coach into the Senate. Theorists theorize that there may have been some die-hard War Eagle Auburn fans working in the nation's capitol and that they pushed for the split ticket vote. "That just makes sense," one source close to the Birmingham office commented. "You need to back your coaches, just like you do your team."

In related news, the alleged woman allegedly phoned to comment that she wondered why she had a flat tire or maybe two at just that moment. "My neighbor's a nice enough man, but he's a die-hard Republican," the alleged woman said. "And he's made friends with my pit bull Fang by feeding him deer meat. He might've sneaked over and flattened that tire while Fang was chomping venison." When reminded that she had previously mentioned two flat tires, the alleged woman replied, "Two, one, what's the difference? I've never been good at math. Some day I'll tell you what happened in my seventh grade math class. Or maybe it was the eighth. See what I mean?"

Updated Update! *Alleged Woman Spotted!* The alleged woman whose Nissan was filled with Biden ballots was caught on film in her back yard at a grill. A private drone flying overhead caught the alleged woman drinking what looked like a cocktail. What appeared to be two cherries floated in the drink, but a little bobbing pink and orange fan kept that exact number uncertain. When the drone flew over again in an attempt to focus, it first appeared that the alleged woman bent to pet her pit bull, but instead she picked up a shotgun. Though the drone did suffer casualties, it was able to limp home.

Breaking News! *Alleged Woman Claims Hunting Mistake!* The alleged woman whose Nissan held either just under or just over seven million fake Biden ballots, called in to this reporter, claiming she thought the wounded drone was a low-flying mallard. "We get all kinds of ducks and quacks around here, because of the pond, you know. Tell that man I'm sorry I hurt his little drone. My pit bull was going wild, so maybe he should apologize to Fang. Is there a peeping-drone law in Alabama? There should be, if there isn't."

Sheriff Brandon "Big" Biggs commented that duck season was over a month away, but there was nothing he could do, since the alleged woman lived in the county, and shooting off a gun there isn't illegal. "Shucks and potato chips, my little boy and two girls do it all the time," he added. When asked if this was his daughter with the ruby ankle bracelet, Sheriff Biggs frowned. "I got work to do," he said.

Update! *Lawyer Files Suit!* Rudy Gullibilliani, a New York lawyer, filed suit in Sumter County Court over the Biden ballots found in the alleged woman's Nissan's trunk. "We just can't have this kind of thing going on, even in some backwater county. Seven and a half million fraudulent, fake ballots for Biden? What are we to make of that? I mean, are there even that many people in this so-called county? And isn't that a dandy coincidence that the supposed popular margin for the supposed winner—you know his name, I don't need to tell you—was seven million?" In court, Mr. Gullibilliani had refused to use the word "fraud," instead claiming that he and the acting President were just acting as concerned citizens concerned for what is best for America and even for Alabama, notwithstanding Jeff Sessions.

Breaking News! *Recount Delayed!* Trained FBI agents from Georgia were hindered by poor lighting and lack of night-vision binoculars, an undisclosed source reported. "Those overhead lights in that fire station were awfully low wattage, is all I can say. Money-savers, I guess. And the glare off that shiny fire truck's chrome didn't help. They must not have many fires, so they sit around and polish, I suppose." To explain, this district of Sumter County employs a volunteer firehouse as its polling station. The agents will return in the morning and open the doors to the station to resume the count, Agent Sam Strong reported. "Sunlight will help," he added. Another source claimed that the lighting in the firehouse had always seemed too bright to her. "But then, they've never let me volunteer as a firewoman, so I may be prejudiced in the matter." When asked if perhaps the males thought a woman firefighter wouldn't be strong enough, the woman hoisted a nearby barrel half-filled with rainwater and toted it fifteen feet to block an entrance door to the station. The woman, who was later identified as Bertha "Twelve-Toes" Biggs (no known relation to Sheriff Biggs), then drove her cardinal red 2 x 4 pick-up off the premises, accidentally tossing gravel on this reporter.

In other news, suspicious movement near Sumter County's western border has been spotted. Mayor Babette "Babes" Babcock and Voting Supervisor Eve Adams both voiced alarm at the movement from nearby Meridian, Mississippi. A caravan of pick-ups was seen leaving the city of Meridian late yesterday afternoon, heading east toward the state line between Mississippi and Alabama. "This is scary," Mayor Babcock told this reporter, "there were gun racks on every one of those pick-ups, from what I've been told." Supervisor Eve Adams then added, "The Governor, she need to get some hustle on about that empty Secretary of Defense position."

News! News! News! *Count Further Delayed!* When local polling volunteers and the special team of Georgia FBI agents showed at the precinct fire station on Wednesday, they found the entrance blocked by a fifty- or fifty-three gallon drum half-filled with rainwater. "I've been told it hasn't rained here for at least ten days," Agent Strong commented. Polling Supervisor Eve Adams added, "It hasn't rained here for thirteen days. And I know. Me and my family live here." Agent Strong indicated that he would call the weather bureau. "You call that Birmingham man all you want. James M. Spann, huh! What's that M stand for? Maybe, maybe not? Last summer he said we was just going to have some iddy-biddy storms and rain. We had two tornadoes! Two, not one, not three! And you think he can count better than me? One of them tornadoes killed my ex-husband, not that he was worth killing. Yanked the gin bottle right from his hand and clonked him with it, right on his useless, hard skull."

By noon, the barrel was moved and the counting re-commenced. Once more, however, it was cut short because of the overhead lighting in the fire station. Agent Strong had wanted to purchase higher wattage bulbs, but the local Wal-Mart reportedly has to process any state or federal purchase order through district channels and that could take up to four days, which would lead into the weekend. The agent then suggested that the trees surrounding the fire station might be felled. “Them are pecan trees!” Supervisor Eve Adams shouted. “Local folks gather pecans every Fall.” Agent Strong apologized. “That’s okay, Hon; you from the city. You didn’t know.”

In related news, the owner of the wounded drone reportedly contacted Rudy Gullibilliani to see whether he might handle a civil suit against the alleged woman for shooting his drone. The damage could be as much as forty-three dollars, but “that doesn’t count the suffering my little boy will go through when he sees this poor, blue, wounded drone.” When contacted, Lawyer Gullibilliani said he was considering the merits of the case.

In other news, Alabama’s governor has still not announced a Secretary of Defense for the state. Red and black and bright yellow pick-ups were spotted congregating near the Alabama-Mississippi line. The lack of a state Secretary of Defense has been cited as prompting this breach. “In normal times, those Meridian, Mississippi, folk know to mind their own soil,” Mayor Babette “Babes” Babcock commented.

Fresh off the Wire! *Ballot Count Confirmed!* After some delay, the special Georgia FBI team and the local voting poll have agreed that there were an even seven million ballots in the trunk of the alleged woman's Nissan. "Not one over, not one under. Seven even million," Agent Strong and Supervisor Eve Adams announced, linking arms. "That's seven million with all those zeroes and no extra numbers," Supervisor Adams added. The two teams appeared amicable as they ate from seven symbolic and celebratory tubs of KFC original recipe chicken. The tubs were provided by local philanthropist Patty "Pearl" Pureheart. "Helping heal harmful hurts hits the hunky happiness button hard for me," Ms. Pureheart commented. "Honest," she added.

In related news, the alleged woman's mask was found hanging in an oak tree on a dirt road near her farm. "We got suspicious when the GPS signal hadn't moved for eighteen hours," Sheriff Biggs commented. "I mean, she's sorter wiry and jumpy and all, and before this, even at midnight she'd be prancing around, doing heaven knows what." Fortunately, the alleged woman called the sheriff's office to admit she'd been climbing the tree with her two nieces, Jilly and Lilly, and the mask got caught. "We considered charging her with damaging county property, but her nieces are friends of my boy, so we dropped those charges. She has a new mask. It's Hunter Red, with some protective cotton around its transmitter in case of falls."

In other news, Alabama's governor has still not announced a Secretary of Defense for the state. As many as three-dozen pick-up trucks have been sighted along

Sumter County's western border. "Maybe those Georgia FBI folk can stop eating chicken long enough to ride over there and give us an accurate count," Mayor Babcock commented. "Someone told me she thought there were four-dozen."

Breaking News! *One More Recount of Ballots Demanded!* Lawyer Gullibilliani has successfully filed a motion to have the Biden ballots recounted. The recount will begin in two days, on a Monday. "This time, I'd like to see some binoculars with night vision provided," the New York lawyer stated, grimacing and wiping the side of his head. A reporter offered him a Kleenex, which he refused. When asked if he were going to represent the drastic drone damage debacle, he said he was certainly considering it.

All the News That's New! *Recount of Recount of Recount?* The seventh or ninth recount (the exact number varies) of the Biden ballots is now underway. The Georgia FBI has been provided with night-vision binoculars thanks to an emergency grant from Montgomery. Agent Strong and Supervisor Adams agreed they would have the recount wrapped up within 24 hours. They joined arms for a photo. It was believed to be the first time a White man and a Black woman have publicly linked arms in the county. A local philanthropist was so pleased she provided coffee and donuts to all involved. Local churches, meanwhile, offered prayers for the safety of those involved. When asked why they were praying for safety, a preacher from the First and Second Half Baptist Church commented that people had been hearing gossip: "There are some Democrats in the mix, after all." His deacon added, "And also some ace of spades n—" the deacon's words were interrupted by a COVID-like cough from the preacher.

Alabama's governor said she thought that the rumors of congregating pick-ups on the state line were exaggerated. "Probably just some Mississippi boys hunting deer. They better have Alabama hunting licenses." Nonetheless, she announced she had narrowed her choice for the Secretary of Defense to two candidates, though she refused to disclose their names.

Breaking Report! *Lawyer Rejects Recount!* Lawyer Rudy Gullibilliani has rejected the twenty-four hour recount that confirmed that an even seven million ballots had been stored in the alleged woman's black Nissan, saying he thought the agents and polling volunteers were either confused or in collusion. To back his latter claim, the lawyer passed out photos of the two groups sharing not only fried chicken, but coffee and donuts. "Some of those donuts were chocolate-coated with those little frosted sparkles," Mr. Gullibilliani added, looking about before wiping the side of his face and inspecting his fingers. The Circuit judge agreed, and a recount has been scheduled for Friday.

The Latest of the Latest! *CDC Involved!* The Atlanta headquarters for the Center for Disease Control has indicated concern about the handling of the alleged seven million Biden ballots, stating that as many as 243 or 252 hands may have individually touched each ballot. "And that's not counting the alleged woman and any cohorts she may have employed," Doctor Herman "Hiccup" Healthman, M.D., iterated. "If those ballots test positive, there's going to be a quarantine." When asked if the quarantine's extent would expand should the ballots prove to be real, Dr. Healthman replied, "If that should ever prove to be the case, we will have a major crisis on hand. That would of course mean that seven million voters had touched the ballots. I don't want anyone to misinterpret this, but let's hope for the sake of a healthy America that those ballots are fake. Either way, I'm preparing a team to test each ballot for COVID-19." When asked what might happen if the ballots test positive, Dr. Healthman replied, "Of course, we will then follow standard procedure and each ballot will be isolated for up to fourteen days. I understand there are only two hospitals in the area, so we may require large field units and triage, as in time of war."

The governor of Alabama has yet to identify her choice for Secretary of Defense.

In related news, campfires have been spotted at night along the Alabama-Mississippi border. Pictures were provided through a private drone owner, who wished to remain anonymous due to advice from his lawyer. When asked who his lawyer was, the unidentified owner responded, "I'm not free to say, but my hair stylist is giving him a free consult."

News Flash! *Proud Bananas Respond!* This weekend, The Proud Bananas, a national political group, offered the following comments about the seven million (or so) ballots the alleged woman toted in her black Nissan's trunk: "If those ballots test so-called positive, we may just save everyone the expense of a field hospital and isolation. We may just ride down to Alabama and eat them, just to prove how silly this plandemic stuff is. I mean, haven't you had a teeny cold before? Did you go crying to a senator and stuffing masks down everyone's throats when you did?"

News Break! *Tire Shop Blowout!* In an exclusive interview to this reporter, Joe "JJ" Jo of JJ's Tire Center reported that he had fit the alleged woman's black Nissan with extra heavy-duty shocks three weeks before the FBI reported the falsified ballots. JJ said of the alleged woman: "She's a wiry piece of work, so I wondered why she wanted them shocks. I get out-of-county bootleggers in now and then wanting them kind of shocks for, well, you know, but she didn't fit that type. Though she did have that mean-eyed pit bull with her. I charged her my usual low rates and mounted those shocks right on that Nissan. We made her take that pit bull out to the back lot. It killed a mole there. It's a awfully vicious dog." JJ of JJ's Tire Center then looked about and leaned toward this reporter, pulling a breath mint from his shirt pocket. "You know, that alleged woman's right: those seven million ballots may have already been in that Nissan's trunk. I had to squirt extra grease into my hydraulic lift to get that car up high enough to replace them shocks. That doesn't put me under suspicion, does it? I mean, the Japanese could have done planted them ballots from the get-go, right? I don't want to wear no ankle bracelet or retard electric implant sissy COVID gas mask, neither one. Go over and arrest Mr. Sony or High Tajimoto, that's what I think."

Hot News and Advice! *Collectible Items?* With the Bogus Biden Ballot case spinning out of control and going viral, this reporter has learned that some folk are printing off all these Internet blasts, in hopes that their future collectible value will increase. If only we had any mullets around here to wrap. Ha. But squirrel meat keeps well in old printer paper, I've been told. Double-ha. Just kidding. Folks, please keep in mind that . . . well . . . that if you want me to autograph any of those printed blasts, I will.

And right here, I'll just add that there is an important update to the JJ Tire Center news, and that comes directly from Agent Strong of the Birmingham FBI:

"We tested that alleged woman's Nissan's shocks first thing. I mean first thing when we were called to fix that flat tire. There was only one flat tire. Our agents go through the rigorous Hoover Number Assessment Protocol. Anyway, the three agents responding reported that the black Nissan's rear-end was slumped down 'like a little girl playing marbles.' Quote and unquote. You know, I can't always keep responsible for my agents. We try to sophisticate them up after the month-long Hoover Number Assessment Protocol, but I guess breeding just takes over now and then. Anyway, the point I'm trying to make is that the alleged woman's Nissan just had regular old factory-issued shock absorbers installed on it, nothing fancy, like Mr. Joe Jo Joey JJ claimed. As I've mentioned before, this part of Alabama in Sumter County is dirt poor and folk down here will do just about anything to grab attention. But as long as this is the last we hear from Mr. Joe 'JJ' Jo Joey, I don't think the Bureau will take any further action, so he needn't worry about an ankle bracelet monitor or such. I got work to do and don't have time for his foolishness. Why's he have that stupid name, anyway?"

In related news, Mayor Babette 'Babes' Babcock has called for volunteers to patrol the Sumter-Lauderdale County lines. "We've always had an uneasy relationship with those Meridian, Mississippi, folk. They're jealous of our resources," the Mayor iterated. "Everyone knows that," she added.

Alabama's governor could not be reached for a timeline concerning the appointment of a new Alabama Secretary of Defense.

Sizzling Hot News! *CDC Seizes Falsifed Biden Ballots!* Just before the FBI and Sumter County Polling officials were set to recount the ballot count, following the circuit court order, following Lawyer Rudy Gullibilliani's renewed suit, CDC officials barged in to test the alleged woman's reported seven million even ballots, with all those zeros. Supervisor Eve Adams commented, "They swooped in like some flock of blackbirds, exceptin' they was dressed in white Hazmat suits. If Agent Strong hadn't of stopped his fine men, I think there might have been shooting. Looked like some moon invasion or somethin' dropping in on our little old volunteer fire station. We all were just jokin' and laughin' and settlin' in to the coffee and donuts that nice woman gave us. You need to put that in your paper or whatever you're using these days and times, so folks don't think we're lollygagging and fine-dining on taxpayer's money."

More Sizzling News! *CDC Claims Ballots Test Positive!* By noon today, nearly a dozen or fifteen (the actual number is uncertain) representatives of the Center for Disease Control in Atlanta had confirmed that over half the Ballistic Biden Ballots taken from the Alleged Woman's Nissan had tested positive for COVID-19 and that the Center further expected a 100% totality of the ballots to do so by this evening, "given the lack of social distancing these ballots have undergone." When asked if the Alleged Woman would need to be placed in quarantine, CDC director Doctor Herman Healthman, M.D., replied, "That's our very next stop. We don't even need to count any further or farther either one to know we have to do that." Sumter County Sheriff Biggs advised that Doctor Healthman send out a drone to ascertain whether the Alleged Woman was home. "Just kidding," Sheriff Biggs added. "But I had better go out there with you."

Breaking News! *Now It's Up North Too!* Pick-up trucks have been spotted near Sumter County's northern border, gathering in Aliceville, Alabama, for over two hours. "At first we thought it was just some of those neo-Nazis scrounging around to see if they could find any leftover swastikas from when German soldiers were held at the POW camp here in our fair city during World War II," an unidentified source commented. "But then," an unidentified friend of the unidentified source broke in, "the boys in these pick-ups bought up all the ammunition in our four gun shops." When the first unidentified source nudged his unidentified friend, the friend admitted, "Well, yeah, that ain't all that unusual, I guess. But they wouldn't order any hamburgers from the Dairy Queen. Not a one. Just sweet iced tea and a big group of milkshakes. Vanilla, no chocolate. You gotta admit that's strange. A woman at the Dairy Queen's counter said she overheard that they were saving their stomachs for some juicy ballards." When this reporter asked if the woman misheard and the visitors might have mentioned, 'Ballots,' the unidentified pair said, "Why sure, that's what they said, 'mallards.' " / "But it ain't duck season, so that ain't right neither," one of them commented on opening a pouch of Red Man. This reporter refused the proffered virgin first chew and instead drove to the Dairy Queen, where she ordered a chocolate-dipped cone and spoke with the counter-person in question. "Yep, 'ballots' is what they said all right. And I got to tell you, the manager don't want those boys back again. They stole all our packets of hot sauce. You think they're gonna use them to spice those ballots?"

News Break! *Mayor Babcock Pleads with Governor!* Mayor Babette "Babes" Babcock just one hour ago in a phone conversation urged that Alabama's governor quickly move on appointing a Secretary of Defense to the open position left by the firing of Tom "Tough" Thompson. Before his dismissal, Secretary Thompson had commented that he felt no interference from surrounding states had influenced the voting process in Alabama this year. He added that radar over the past sixteen or twenty-two months had found no untoward incursion from Tennessee, Georgia, or Mississippi. "Even that Arkansas sliver was clean," the then Secretary had claimed. The Governor had previously stated that she felt certain surrounding states were unduly trying to influence our senatorial race, especially.

According to Mayor Babcock, the governor has assured her the position would be filled by Friday. "That's two days away, though, so I'm continuing the call for volunteers to patrol our western border. I also asked the governor how long she was going to keep the mask mandate going. You know a lot of county residents have bought red bandannas and are wearing them now. I'm not sure if it's in support of that Alleged Woman or to make fun of her. She's got some friends, but she's got some enemies. Whatever, it's making our Sheriff and the Livingston City Police Chief awful nervous, on top of all those pick-ups and night fires over there. And now this stuff about Aliceville to top the top of that top of it all."

No Braking for the Breaking News! *Proud Bananas Make Announcement!* A spokesman for the famed national movement called the Proud Bananas has indicated the group's intent to kidnap the COVID-19 ballots that recently tested positive. "We're gonna eat every last one of those ballots and prove once and for all that this COVID stuff is just that—stuff. The Proud Bananas ain't yellow. The Proud Bananas are hard and white! We're gonna take pleasure in chewing every last one of those ballots up. I mean, gnashing, ripping with our white teeth! Maybe put some hot sauce on them. And we ain't gonna do no quarantine afterward, neither. We're driving our trucks and motorcycles back and kiss and hug our girlfriends like good white Proud Bananas. I got to tell you, frankly, that the Proud Bananas are disappointed with the Alabama chapter of the KKK. I was talking with their Super Blue Dragon Wizard Gecko fella, and you know what he said? He said they don't have much luck down in Sumter County because there's so many . . . well, lady, you're with that fake news stuff so you wouldn't print what he said. But I can tell you he didn't say it's because there's so many fire ants down there. You just let them Sumter people know we're coming. The Proud Bananas ain't yellow! The Proud Bananas are white! The Proud Bananas are going to eat every last one of those COVID-19 ballots. Gnash 'em!"

Latest News! *Alleged Woman Breaks Silence!* The Alleged Woman accused of toting seven million split tickets for Biden / Tommy T. Tubbs in her Nissan has broken silence. "If that Atlanta doctor is going to quarantine me, is he going to pay my light and gas bills? Is he going to put groceries on my table? What about Thanksgiving and a turkey? My sister always brings her two girls over. Sometimes my second cousin brings her two boys over. Kissing cousins, so we gotta watch them, if you know what I mean. And my mom! She's retired now, with no more stamps, no more of those nylon-plastic trays we used to set tomato plants out in. You know, I only have so many shotgun shells left, and the squirrel and rabbit around here are already scarce. I don't think drones would have much taste. Ha. And say, just when am I gonna get my car back? When? I see them FBI people and them polling place people eating away on fried chicken in that fire station—you want to step inside and look at *my* table? Ho, Fang! That's okay, Fang, back off and let the nice lady come on in and look at how bare our table is. Fang! No, Fang! No! Down! Well hell, just take my word: there ain't even turnips on that kitchen table. It's pre-Civil War. My great-great-great-great granddaddy carved it. Got some Confederate blood on one of the legs, from Sherman or some other big general in the battle just north of here. They hold a right interesting re-creation up there in Gainesville. Cannons and lots of racket. Folks dressed up in Blue and folks dressed up in Gray. People ought to go. You think you might want to buy the table, Lady? Fang, damn your hide! Down! No!"

Breaking News That Is Never Broken! *Door Once More Blocked!* While Sumter Sheriff Biggs reportedly escorted Dr. Herman "Hiccup" Healthman, M.D., and his team to the Alleged Woman's house to inform her of the quarantine restrictions, FBI Agent Sam Strong and Poll Supervisor Eve Adams reportedly commandeered the fire station's fire truck and drove off to the Demopolis KFC for "counting provisions." The remaining volunteers and agents claimed that it was such a fine autumn day that they went walking toward the river. The Biden Ballots had been wrapped in sanitary plastic and left on four pallets in front of the fire station. "We didn't see any danger in leaving them out in the sunshine with a nice spray of bleach over the plastic. I mean, no one is dumb enough to drink that bleach, even down here in the boondocks," a poll volunteer later volunteered.

Not even just one hour later, however, the door to the firehouse had once more been blocked with a rain barrel, now completely filled with water. There reportedly was a note attached to the barrel that read, *Call me if you need some help movin' this. You Know Whom. XXXOOO. P&S. I learned my arithmetic plenty of times, so I can help count too. And, no, I don't really have twelve toes. Just because I'm big, doesn't mean I'm weird. That's a stupid rumor spread by some mad ex-boyfriend. Hurt his dinky feelings because I wouldn't, well . . . you know, do that other thing.*

Agent Sam Strong said that he arrived first and read the note aloud to gathering folk. When someone asked if there was any special symbolism in the word 'whom,' Agent Strong explained that it was citified grammar. "But I don't think we can blame any of my Georgia agents for this. And that Atlanta CDC crew is all out quarantining the Alleged Woman." / "Probably collectin' some buck-shot in their butts," Supervisor Eve Adams interrupted. This busy reporter arrived at that moment. Supervisor Adams looked at her and asked, "You pass anyone suspicious? Like maybe Bertha 'Twelve-Toes' Biggs?" On giving a small nod and nose wiggle, this reporter was then confronted with myriad questions, including the accusation that Bertha Biggs was a fifth cousin on her mother's side. Which just isn't true. This reporter cannot speak to the number of toes Ms. Biggs might be in possession of. That foul rumor has gotten plenty of circulation over the years. You might say that no one has been able to give those toes the boot. Ha.

Breaking News! *Shots Reported!* Dr. Herman Healthman, M.D., of the Atlanta CDC, reported that buckshot whizzed over the heads of him and his seven or nine assistants when they approached the house of the Alleged Woman. "I looked around for Sheriff Biggs, but he was standing about one hundred meters away behind a pecan tree." When asked just how far that was in yards or feet, Dr. Healthman commented, "I don't have time for foolish questions. I have work to do."

More Breaking News! *More Shots Reported!* On the western side of Sumter County, shots played out for over an hour this afternoon. "Sounded like it was New Year's Eve or like maybe Cuba and them Castro brothers took to boats and invaded Biloxi," a local farmer commented. "It was guns, all right," his wife commented. "I heard a 30.06, a Remington .410, a whole big bunch of nine-millimeters, and some .357s shooting." The farmer then added, "My wife, she knows her guns, so I expect there was all of those in the mix." The wife went on, "Some .38 specials, maybe, and a couple of twelve gauge. May even have been a air rifle once or twice, some kid joining in the fun."

More and More Breaking News! *More and More Shots Reported!* In the north Sumter County town of Gainesville, shots were heard during the night. Gainesville Mayor Jesse Jim James commented that it sounded like the annual Civil War reenactment the city puts on. "But it's not that time of year," he added. "Folks ought to come out and see that reenactment, though. It's a real doozy. Folks dressed up in Blue and Gray and all." When asked to further explain the nighttime shots, Mayor James replied, "I can't. It's a mystery. But folks ought to come out and see that reenactment. It's a doozy."

The Latest of the Latest News! *Lawyer Gullibilliani Demands Secure Lockdown!* New York City lawyer Rudy Gullibilliani has accused the FBI and the Sumter polling supervisor of collusion. "Those ballots are just lying in front of that firehouse. Anyone—even a Democrat—could figure out how to get them and mix them up with real ballots, claim they were just found on the side of the building or something. Maybe in a spittoon. This is that kind of place, I'm telling you. But no matter where the place is, we need a true election. We don't need any fraudulent election. America needs to be sure of its next President, needs to be sure that the next President is who and whom Americans truly elected. If you let them get away with seven million ballots this year, what's it going to be next election? Seven million and ten? Seven million and twenty? Instead of the trunk of a Nissan, is it going to be the trunk of Buick? I know crooks very well, and I can tell you this is exactly what will happen. This country doesn't need excuses and crooks. This country needs truth." Mr. Gullibilliani was standing on a wooden step stool before the Sumter County firehouse and the five pallets of alleged ballots that the Alleged Woman reportedly toted in the trunk of her black Nissan. Mr. Gullibilliani wiped the side of his head several times. When a reporter reached to offer him Kleenex, he scowled. He later was heard to say under his breath, "Was a mistake climbing up on that stool. Heat rises. How do these yahoos stand it down here? It's November and I think my hair's melting."

A Sumter judge concurred with Mr. Gullibilliani and ordered the five pallets moved inside the station for security reasons. Local volunteer fire chief Red "Ruddy" Scarlet bemoaned the fact that their faithful three-year old fire engine would have to sit out in the elements to make room for the ballots. "Is that darned city lawyer gonna get us a big tarp? I wish he'd fallen off that darned stool and bumped the other side of his bleeding head on the gravel. Why's his head bleeding anyway? Or maybe it's not blood? Maybe it's some new citified brand of dandruff shampoo? All I'm saying is that the boys are right fond of that engine. It's got a loud siren and a bunch of lights. And there's this big yellow warning gauge so's we can't never leave the station without hoses again."

In other news, the Alabama governor has announced that she will announce the new Secretary of Defense tomorrow at noon.

"About time," Livingston Mayor Babette Babcock commented.

Late Night News! *Where's the Stamps?* This reporter received a note from a Concerned Citizen wondering just what in the world had happened to all the booklets of Elvis stamps. The note was tied around an old shock absorber and tossed in an open window. When this suspicious reporter immediately called both Ms. Eve Adams and Mr. Sam Strong, she was told they were "occupied." Sadly, this reporter has often enough noticed the same sign displayed over Port-o-lets at the state fair.

In other news, Lawyer Rudy Gullibilliani has reversed course and claims that he will represent the Alleged Woman in a civil action lawsuit against both the alleged drone owner and Dr. Herman Healthman of the Atlanta CDC. "Trespass, invasion of privacy, mental anguish, harmful harm, minor mayhem, and tax evasion." When asked how tax evasion fit in, Lawyer Gullibilliani wiped his head and replied he didn't say that. "What I said was, 'Ask away then.' " / "But nobody was asking," this reporter commented, offering Mr. Gullibilliani a perfumed Kleenex for the side of his head, which was oozing brown liquid. "At least it ain't a blowfly traipsing around up there," one of the poll volunteers commented.

The Alleged Woman was unavailable for immediate response about Mr. Gullibilliani's representing her, though a neighbor commented, "I'd be surprised if she'd let that damned Yankee sonofabitch drip-faced lawyer kiss her pit bull's ass."

News Break! *Lawyer Gullibilliani Clarifies!* New York lawyer Rudy Gullibilliani, locally known as "The Sneer," has announced that he will be representing both the Alleged Woman and the owner of the drone allegedly damaged by shotgun pellets when flying over the Alleged Woman's house. "It's time for a new approach to justice," the lawyer said in answer to a question as to the legality of representing both opposing sides in a single case. "And what better time to bring that approach forward than now. I know the law very well," he concluded.

A local accountant speculated that Mr. Gullibilliani was hedging his bets in case President Trumpet once more declares bankruptcy and is unable to pay him. "The beauty of taking both sides in a civil case like this, is that the lawyer is assured of collecting a contingency fee either way. I'm going to recommend that my daughter, who's fresh out of UA's law school, start doing this. I'll have to think how it might apply to CPA's."

In other news, the Governor of Alabama is set to announce a new Secretary of Defense within the hour.

In related other, other news, overnight rain evidently doused campfires spotted on the Alabama-Mississippi border, and the Gainesville Dairy Queen reportedly sold out of vanilla ice cream, though there are still several gallons of sweet tea brewing. "Whoever these fellas are, they sure like their vanilla," the store's owner commented.

Breaking News! *Local High School Project!* A teacher of a local high school science class says his class plans a project to prove that drones have rights. "They've got feelings, anyone can see that," one student commented as the teacher looked on. "We're going to prove it, and then we're forming the first chapter for the SPCD, Society for the Prevention of Cruelty to Drones." Another student stepped forward to add, "A nice woman philothropist has donated enough money for the project and for donuts and Coca-Colas. We might include computers in with drones, too, you know. Computers can talk to you, you know. They have feelings too. Lots of them. A friend of mine said that once her computer asked her out on a date. She didn't go, though."

Breaking News! *From the Capitol!* The Governor of Alabama has announced her choice for Alabama's Secretary of Defense, a position left empty after the governor fired the last secretary. Jean "Jennie" Highjeans will fill the position immediately, the governor announced, and she will immediately begin securing Alabama's borders. Secretary Highjeans gave a brief statement saying, "There has been concern over both our western border with Mississippi and recently our northern border with Tennessee. Our eastern border is safe, as our relation with Georgia has always been secure, and now with those special agents counting ballots over in Sumter County, we just feel really good about that border. And of course, our southern border has always been amicable toward the oysters and fish." Three people in the crowd of eight or nine laughed. Secretary Highjeans has long been known in government circles for her rollicking sense of humor.

This Just In! *Sumter County Circuit Court Injuncts!* Sumter County Circuit Court has agreed to grant an injunction sought by Rudy Gullibilliani that would require a recount of the ballots that the Alleged Woman toted in the trunk of her black Nissan Altima. Mr. Gullibilliani has demanded that Hazmat suits and night vision binoculars be provided to all involved so that the count might be quickly confirmed. "Truth is what we want. Truth is all we want. I've known some truthful people." When asked to elaborate, Lawyer Gullibilliani wiped his cheek. No one offered Mr. Gullibilliani a Kleenex, though spectators held up cell phones for a photo opp. Mr. Gullibilliani sneered, though he later claimed, "That was a smile. It was a New York City smile. I always smile, you know. I've known some friendly people."

Breaking News! *Blowback on Gubernatorial Appointment!* Mayors in several large Alabama cities have questioned the appointment of a female as Secretary of Defense, but Livingston Mayor Babette Babcock has indicated complete confidence. "I rode in a tank with her one Independence Day. She was driving and let me shoot off the cannon." When asked if she hit the target, Mayor Babcock replied, "I need to get to work. We have to secure our border."

Newsbreak! *Proud Banana Group Speaks!* The leader of the Proud Bananas announced that the group was going to remain in Gainesville for an additional day. "There's no rush, since those fools down in Sumter County are worried about special suits. Huh. Like White suits with scuba tanks can prevent a plandemic. I'm telling you, we are going to eat all those supposedly COCKVID ballots and then drive on back up to Michigan. Anyone who wants to ride with us is welcome." A local teenager with violet hair and three nose rings was seen standing behind the leader. "He's . . . he's . . . he's so . . . so brave and so . . . so White," she was heard to comment to a nearby girlfriend.

Breaking News! *Entrance Again Blocked!* The entrance to Sumter County's Volunteer Fire Station #4 was once more found to be blocked by a barrel filled with rainwater. There were no notes on the barrel. One onlooker speculated that the absence of a note might be because of all the raccoons in the area. "Raccoons will carry away just about anything. Except maybe greasy hair dye or blowflies." When this reporter inspected the barrel, she did notice a residue on the barrel's edge that could have indicated Scotch Tape once held down something like a handwritten note.

Ten or thirteen men finally shifted the barrel away, so they could enter the building. The ballots were found safely in place directly over the oil slick left by the fire engine. "That's from the old engine," the volunteer fire chief said. "Not Engine Number 14, which we bought three years ago." / "It was four years ago, Chief," a volunteer who'd shown up to oil the entrance door's hinges commented. / "Hell, three, four, eight. Maybe we can get some of these Georgia folks to count out for us," the chief replied.

New Old News! *Confirmed Count Confirmed!* By evening, the Georgia FBI and the Sumter polling volunteers had combined to confirm the count of an even seven million ballots. Rudy Gullibilliani complained that the Hazmat suits provided for his people overseeing the count had hazy visors. Alabama's new secretary of Defense, Jean "Jennie" Highjeans, commented that the visors were "Hazy, not Hazmatty." Several people gathered around laughed. The new secretary, known for her sense of humor, was on site to investigate the rumored gathering of pick-ups on Sumter County's western border with Mississippi. She said she also planned on traveling to Gainesville in the morning to investigate a rumored Proud Banana gathering.

Rudy Gullibilliani commented that low jokes and other tricks like this were just what he expected. "I'll be in court tomorrow. We'll get the true count yet. Don't plan on going back to Georgia for Thanksgiving, is all I can tell those agents."

Breaking News! *Proud Bananas Visit Emelle!* The national group known as The Proud Bananas circled their pick-ups around the entrance to the nation's largest hazardous waste site this morning, giving high-fives to incoming eighteen-wheelers hauling in waste. "This is what America is about. Good things happen when truckers move," the spokesman for The Proud Bananas commented. A young woman with violet hair and three or four nose rings—the number varied as the morning light hit her face—clasped the spokesman's arm, which displayed the blood red tattoo "Freeedom." As the spokesman flexed his biceps, the three e's in the word were seen to jump. "It was almost like they were dancing a heebie-jeebies song," an onlooker commented. "Very entertaining. The fella should get on a reality show."

From the highway, Sheriff Biggs lifted a pair of discarded non-night vision binoculars to study the girl with the violet hair. "She's only got three nose rings," the sheriff confirmed. "But I counted six rings in her right ear and another six in her left. I figure she's got a ring for each year old she is. That makes fourteen, doesn't it?" When someone commented that it came to fifteen, Sheriff Biggs responded, "Math. Who can stand it? Fourteen or fifteen, I can't do anything unless her parents complain or unless that Banana totes her over the state line. And then I can't do anything anyway, because they're over the state line. From the looks of those nose- and ear- rings, I'm guessing her parents might just be glad to see her gone. There's a wind coming up. I hope they keep those COVID-19 ballots under wraps. It'd be a terrible thing to have them blowing loose around, kids pawing them and all."

Big Late News Views! *Secretary Arrives!* Alabama Secretary's of Defense arrived in Gainesville early this morning to find that The Proud Bananas had left before dawn for Emelle. Two big city mayors commented that this was "about what they expected from a female Secretary of Defense." Mayor Babette "Babes" Babcock countered that, "Anyone can get some wires crossed now and then. You should of seen her driving that tank."

Update! Update! *A Dire Warning!* Doctor Anthony Stephen Fauci of the National Institute of Allergy and Infectious Diseases has warned that congregating—even in pick-ups—could spread COVID-19. He added that the half-life of the virus on paper, especially on porous paper such as employed in voting ballots, has yet to be ascertained. He further urged all to take care as the holidays and especially Thanksgiving quickly approach. "Some poorer counties in this country might be tempted to employ used ballots as dinner napkins on Thanksgiving. Please, please, please don't do this. We just don't know."

In response, Patty "Pearl" Pureheart, a local philanthropist, has ordered twenty pallets of Wal-Mart's best Everyday Paper Napkins to be given away at four distribution points throughout Sumter county on the day before Thanksgiving.

Alabama's Secretary of Defense, Jean Highjeans, commented, "Pallets are a lot safer than ballots." Four people laughed at her joke. "I got work to do. I need to get on down to Emelle as well. There was nothing to gain in Gainesville." Three people in the listening crowd laughed. Jean Highjeans has long been noted for her sense of humor.

In other news, the Alleged Woman was spotted with two teenagers flying a drone over Highway 28. The drone was trailing vapor behind. “It looked like it was some wounded bird doing a loop-de-loop,” one witness said, speaking from his stand selling barbecued ribs. / “You mean, Dad, like maybe it was crying out, trying to talk to us?” his daughter asked, holding up a platter of corn on the cob. / “I wouldn’t carry things that far.” / “Well, our science project will show the truth. We’re asking that New York man to come and tell us some truth.” / “Good luck on that,” a passing woman commented. “How long do you smoke those ribs? They sure smell good.”

Late Developing News Break! *Surprise Star Speaker!* In a surprise visit, Lawyer Rudy Gullibilliani visited Sumter County High School this Tuesday and addressed the student body of three hundred and twenty or twenty-two in the gymnasium. “I’ve always had a soft spot in my heart for drones,” Mr. Gullibilliani droned. “I know drones very well. People say I don’t, but I can assure you three hundred and twenty-five young people I do.”

In other news, Alabama’s Secretary of Defense and an escort of seven or maybe nine personnel carriers from the Alabama National Guard traveled to Emelle. The plant manager of the nation's largest hazardous waste dump greeted them, saying that the cohort of Proud Bananas had left at dawn. When asked what direction they had headed in, the manager pointed south and replied, "They seemed like nice enough people. I think you should try to talk with them." Secretary Highjeans lifted her dark sunglasses and blinked. "I just have to wonder if talking appeals to bananas," she said. "Appeals," she repeated. "Bananas. Appeals." The secretary replaced her dark glasses and entered the lead personnel carrier, shaking her head at the silent manager.

Breaking Report! *TikTok Duo Perform Ballot Bounce!* In an 84 second-long clip, two Sumter County teenagers have taken the TikTok world by storm within just two or three hours by performing what they dubbed the *Ballistic Biden Ballot Bounce*. "We had no idea this would happen," Erin "Ireful" Eire commented. Her partner, Jesse "Jouncy" Jackson agreed, adding, "We were just funning around, making some weird faces like that New York guy that visited our high school yesterday." Erin then added, "It only took us five minutes to get our hair dye to run. We balanced it so that Jesse's ran down his left cheek and mine ran down my right. The hardest part was the faces. Jesse said I looked like the Phantom of the Opera, but we cleaned it up, so that a stretchy smile was the end result. We don't believe in politics. We just want everyone to be happy," Erin concluded. Jesse added, "Yeah, happiness. True that. That's why we don't believe in politics."

Within two or four hours of the interview, the teenage duo had over 60 thousand pings.

In related news, Rudy Gullibilliani has urged the two teens to talk with him before signing any contracts. "I know crooks very well," Mr. Gullibilliani commented. "Those two kids need some good, clear, honest counsel. I remember seeing them yesterday in the gym, up front on the sixth or eighth row. I thought to myself, 'Those two kids are going somewhere.' "

Somewhere and elsewhere, Alabama's Secretary of Defense and seven or nine personnel carriers from the Alabama National Guard were spotted on a back road in Sumter County. It appeared that one of the personnel carriers had slipped into a ditch and that the Secretary and her escort were awaiting a local wrecker service. Joe "JJ" Jo of JJ's Tire Center, commented that his new wrecker was called out of the shop early in the morning. "I'm not saying we helped pull that National Guard vehicle from a ditch, but I'm not saying we didn't either."

Breaking News! *Philanthropist to Provide Turkey*

and Dressing for Family. Family members of the Alleged Woman will be treated to a twenty-one or -four pound Turkey on Thanksgiving, as local philanthropist Patty "Pearl" Pureheart promised the bird will be baked and delivered at eleven or twelve a.m. Thanksgiving Day. "I just can't make a promise on the time of delivery and the weight of the bird. That's math, and you just can't never be sure that stuff."

Breaking News! *Pre-weekend Counting Resumed.* With the overnight special delivery arrival of thirty-seven or thirty-nine special Hazmat suits with Plexiglas double vision visors and accompanying night vision binoculars, counting at Sumter County Fire Station Number Four (Some sources claim it is really Sumter County Station Number Five, as the old station burned down, but was never rebuilt.) has resumed. Each ballot is reportedly being sprayed with bleach and left in the sun for twenty-seven or twenty-nine seconds. "One thing's for certain," Secretary of Defense Jean Highjeans commented, coughing and wiping her dark sunglasses with a nearby Wal-Mart Everyday Paper Napkin, and hesitating as two onlookers joined the listening crowd. "One thing's for certain," she repeated, refitting her dark sunglasses and coughing as wind shifted and bleach spritzed through the air. "One thing." Though the crowd backed away as the Secretary continued to cough, they still seemed eager to hear what frolic the secretary might evoke. The secretary coughed once more, readjusted her sunglasses, and said, "I don't have time for questions. I've got important business in front of me." Listeners appeared disappointed that the secretary had told no joke, for they walked away shaking their heads.

In Sumter Circuit Court, Rudy Gullibilliani asked that the entire ballot count for Candidate Joe Biden be thrown out. When reminded that the seven million ballots had never been delivered and therefore could not be thrown out, Gullibilliani replied, "They're sitting down in the middle of that voting precinct's fire station. Right now! I have photos of them! We can't allow the nineteen electoral votes for the entire state of Alabama to be fraudulently stolen and given over to the Biden camp." When the judge countered that Alabama has only nine electoral votes, Mr. Gullibilliani responded, "That's more than enough! Every American vote is precious! I know crooks very well. We can't allow them to be stolen! We just can't!" The presiding judge stared momentarily at the courtroom's vaulted ceiling as if searching for a blowfly or maybe an oozing brown stain. He then shook his head and asked whether Counsel meant that the crooks should not be stolen or some other, more celestial matter was in jeopardy of theft. At that, Mr. Gullibilliani wiped his head and replied, "Your honor, I have another case pending, concerning damage to a drone and invasion of privacy and maybe even malfeasance. I'm a very busy man. I'd like to turn to that matter if we may."

The court was recessed for lunch and chocolate milk shakes, a favorite of the presiding judge.

Breaking News! *Proud Bananas Camp by River!* The Proud Bananas were spotted camped on the chalk cliffs of the Tombigbee River, near Fort Tombecbee. "This place is a real trip and a half," a leader for the group explained. "All this White! We're going to stay here until the bleach on those Sumter County ballots dries off. We've been following that story on the Internet. We've been stopping at Dairy Queens and collecting their hot sauce to put on those COVIDALIZED ballots. We were told there was a Dairy Queen in Sumterville, but there ain't. Sure are lots of pretty girls around, though. Say hey, what do we say, fellas?" When the spokesman turned and flexed his tattooed biceps, the group called out, "Proud Bananas! We ain't yellow! We're white and hard!"

In related news, Alabama's Secretary of Defense, Jean Highjeans, is reportedly going to meet with the Proud Bananas this afternoon. "I'm going to talk with them about their ballot intent, whether it's Nutcracker or not." When no one laughed, Secretary Jean Highjeans blinked. "Nutcracker. Ballot. Nutcracker. Ballot," she repeated.

Sometimes the Secretary stretches a bit, even for Alabama.

Livingston Mayor Babette "Babes" Babcock, however, commented that she had utmost faith in the newly appointed Secretary. "She can steer a tank like nobody's business. And when she gets those dark glasses on, look out. Funny . . . hoo-whee! She'll have those Bananas and those Meridian folk giggling like teenage girls. I'm not worried at all."

Since last week's rain and the cold snap, no campfires have been spotted on Sumter County's western border. One cattle rancher commented, "Those Meridian fellas are weak-kneed like that. A little rain, a little cold, they run back to Momma."

Breaking News! *Conflicting Ballot Recount!* The latest ballot recount fell two or four short of seven million, that is six million, nine hundred ninety-nine thousand, nine hundred ninety-six or seven or eight. "I knew that Alleged Woman couldn't fit no seven million of these suckers in the trunk of her car," a polling volunteer who demanded his name be withheld commented. Agent Sam Strong later responded, "I think the bleach made two of those ballots clump together. I mean four, sticking so they turned into two. That would account for the shortage. The shortage of two, I mean. Our agents, you know, they go through a rigorous training period in counting. We've got some secret memory devices that we use too. So, I'm saying it's the CDC coming over here with all that bleach that messed the count up. We had that count right the fifth or seventh time, I guarantee it." Polling supervisor Eve Adams stood beside Agent Strong and agreed. "Agent Strong wouldn't tell no falsehoods. He's a man of honor," she commented. "And that's not all."

Turkey Day! *A Day to Eat and Rest!* The President pardoned a turkey named Tomàs today on what could be seen of the White House lawn. Though onlookers had to climb stepladders to take photos over the concertina wire, they claimed it was worth it. "The President looked so kind as he bent to pardon Tomàs," a supporter said. "It was sorta like he was leaning and telling some illegal alien Mexican street urchin that everything would be okay as soon as they found his momma and daddy and some tacos. I mean, my heart just fluttered. The President looks so kind when he leans forward."

The Latest on the Latest! *Alleged Woman and Family Sick!* The entire extended family of the Alleged Woman has taken down sick, a neighbor reported. "We found them late Thanksgiving Day," he said. "Their pit bull come over—at first I thought one of my bitches was in heat, because that Fang pit bull of hers likes his delights, I guess you could say. Must have sired over three hundred pups in this area. Or maybe even three hundred and ten. Darwin, you know about him, right? Surviving with fitness? Sounds like some health nut guru, don't he? Well, that Fang is living, four-legged proof. Of fitness and surviving both. Anyway, none of my doggie ladies were in heat, so my boy and me and the wife followed Fang back to the Alleged Woman's and her momma's house. We called out real loud a bunch, because that Alleged Woman is wiry and quick to pull out a shotgun, you know. No response. We called out to her momma, who's turned a lot quieter since she's retired from that postal job. You should of seen her back when folks had to lick them stamps. Sick all the time, it's as true as I'm standing before you. Tongue-and-spit-germs here, tongue-and-spit-germs there. Anyway, we called and called. No response. Fang started to whine. Now, that ain't like Fang, I got to tell you. It ain't like Fang at all. The gate was open, and so was the back door. There were flies and wasps about it, flitting in and out. My wife spotted one of the little teenage nieces—one of them that climbed up that tree where the Alleged Woman got her electronic mask hung—one of the little Jilly and Lilly nieces holding her tummy and rocking on the kitchen floor inside. Fang went on in and licked her right on the mouth. My wife screamed—she don't trust pit bulls, but they're as sweet as honeyed sugar water most of the time—she screamed, but Fang kept on licking. I mean, he wasn't gnawing or biting or ripping or tearing or anything. So we decided to go on inside too, and see what we could see after calling out a couple more times, just to make sure. About the shotgun and all. Well, I'm telling you: all eight or maybe all ten of them were on the floor holding their stomachs and groaning. 'Go on home and fetch the seltzer water,' my wife told our boy. He did, and when he come back, we gave a dose to all eight or maybe ten of them. I think they're going to be okay. That's what happens when folks push their nose in other folks's business and buy them a bunch of turkey and oyster dressing and giblet gravy and green beans and yams and sweet potato pie and Cool Whip when all those folks have been eating for years is mustard greens with squirrel and rabbit. Do-gooders! Puh-tooey!"

The neighbor went on to explain that the Alleged Woman was unable to respond, other than rocking and holding her stomach. When he offered another shot of seltzer water, the same neighbor reported that she reached back for a bottle of Old Forester. "She nearly clonked herself on the head fetching it," he commented. "I had a snort with her."

Breaking News! *A Fact-Filled Weekend!* Events happened so fast and furious this weekend that this reporter's pretty head is spinning. First, a large group of pick-up trucks once more gathered on the Sumter-Lauderdale border. As many as one hundred-and-four or -six pick-up trucks created a large defensive circle in Mississippi. The alleged trucks claimed they were careful not to violate any treaties and cross into Alabama territory, though one lifelong Sumter resident said he watched as three bright red trucks scraped bark off a water oak that had marked the state line for "just about forever and one or two days." No reason was given for the encamped and circled trucks. "Circles make the tightest and strongest container," the lifelong resident went on to comment. "I don't need no math nor geometry teacher to learn me that. Chickens don't lay square eggs, do they? Or triangles. Or cubes. My brother tried to patent round ice cube trays once. The trays weren't round, the ice cubes were. Or would have been, if he'd gotten that patent. Say, you know why you never see them? Ha. Because they melt! Ha." When asked why he thought the trucks were circling, he responded, "Hell, it ain't none of my business. Go ask them. I do agree with that Livingston Mayor woman, though: Mississippi people are plum jealous of what we got over here in Alabama."

Elsewhere, the Proud Bananas have left the Fort Tombecbee area. A private drone spotted dust rising on Alabama Back Road 443 or 4, and this has been presumed to indicate the location of the Banana group. Three teenage daughters from Sumterville reportedly left with the

Bananas. A local tattoo artist said the three were his best steady customers, but then indicated that, "For the two days those Banana Boys hung around here, I made enough money to take the rest of this year off and do some fancy Christmas shopping too. Hell, I'm going to a Mall, none of this online crap for me. I want to hold what I'm buying. My old lady feels the same. We like to hold things, get a feel for how it's going to work around the house and the yard, see if it'll fit our plans and stuff. Be comfortable and smell right, you know? Anyway, there'll be more little girls growing up in Sumterville. I got my eye on five already, two of them sisters."

In other news, Secretary of Defense Jean Highjeans called for more Alabama National Guard personnel carriers and two tanks. "The situation here is growing serious, so I'll give thanks for those tanks, and tanks for the thanks," she commented. Several onlookers laughed. The secretary has long been known for her sense of humor.

"Hot dang!" Mayor Babette "Babes" Babcock commented when she learned of the incoming tanks. "Tanks! Hot damned dang. Excuse my French."

Rudy Gullibilliani has offered to represent the Alleged Woman in a bodily assault case against local philanthropist Patty "Pearl" Pureheart. He also said he has contacted Ms. Pureheart to represent her, too, for Defamation of Character and Lack of Appreciation. "This is a new age in the courts. We can't stick to the old, tired, muddy ways. It's up to lawyers to pave the way for truth. This election was stolen. Lots of things get stolen, right out of good American pockets. With a new breed of lawyers like myself, matters will straighten out. I know crooks very well, and they don't like this new breed of lawyer. He scares them."

And ever elsewhere, Sumter County High School celebrated its most famous students, "The TikTok Duo," as they have come to be called. The high school's band played a song that the two danced to. The news station from Meridian, Mississippi, sent a camera crew over. Everyone was polite to the crew, and there were no incidents, though the Mississippi folk reportedly focused a good deal on the high school's trophy case. "It's got a good double lock on it," the school's principal assured everyone as the crew drove off. "And that glass isn't really glass, it's bulletproof Plexiglas, you know. We got it on special purchase before this COVID stuff. Hell, you can't touch Plexiglas these days."

And at the Sumter County Fire Station in Coatopa, this: "I suppose we ought to go ahead and say it," Supervisor Eve Adams stated as industrial fans and heaters were turned on to separate and dry the Biden Ballots. Agent Sam Strong grunted and moved one of the fans until it blew on him. "Don't you think we owe it to the people who support us, Sam? Don't you think they'll be happy for us?" the supervisor asked. The agent's head was rotating in time with the fan. "He's counting the revolutions," Supervisor Adams stated. "He does that to keep in practice so's he won't make mistakes on the job. He's so . . . so committed." Supervisor Adams let out a sigh that riffled some of the ballots. "Oh, Sam, I just can't hold it any longer. Everyone, listen! We're engaged! Sam and me, I mean. We're going to get married on Inauguration Day come January! Isn't that swell?"

And with more elsewhere, the Alleged Woman and her nieces Jilly and Lilly were spotted practicing dive-bombing with two drones. "My momma finally cashed her last paycheck from the post office and bought me and my nieces, Jilly and Lilly, this extra toy. We're learning to fly them in attack formation, just so's . . . well, I've been advised not to say why, by this man from New York. My close neighbor says he's got a sneer worse than Fang and that what's left of his hair drips axle grease like his old Ford tractor used to do. Not the lawyer's tractor—he likely never owned or even drove one—but my neighbor's. Still, he is a lawyer and all. Not my neighbor. He's not a lawyer. He hates lawyers. He says he'll coldcock the New York sonofabitch if he steps a left or right foot near his house." The two nieces giggled and landed the two drones. "We've got a surprise for everyone. I didn't think it up, Jilly and Lilly here did. They're not identical twins, but they want to be. They're my nieces. It's an important and smart surprise, isn't it, girls?"

Meanwhile, at the Sumter County fire station, Dr.

Herman Healthman, M.D., worried that the fans and space heaters drying the Ballistic Biden Ballots might be spreading COVID 19 germs. “That virus likes heat. Of course, it may like the cold too, and that’s going to be a problem later on. I sure wish people had stuck to canned sardines in mustard for Thanksgiving. Maybe some fruitcake and low sodium V-8 juice. There wouldn’t have been no overly large gatherings then, you can bet. But well, you know, it is what it is.”

Elsewhere, philanthropist Patty “Pearl” Pureheart stated that the four distribution points for the free Wal-Mart Everyday Paper Napkins were so successful that she’s going to expand to six or eight points for Christmas and order another truckload of napkins. “I just wish that the Alleged Woman, her mother, and her extended family had taken a little time to use those napkins between bites. Instead of gulping down that twenty-three or -four pound turkey and getting themselves so sick.”

“Instead of gobbling the gobbler, they should have napped with napkins,” Secretary Jean Highjeans was heard to respond. Several listeners laughed. The Secretary has long been known for her sense of humor.

Lastly, Rudy Gullibilliani showed at Coatopa, Sumter County Fire Station Number Four or Thirteen late on Sunday afternoon. “I’m thinking the President might send some pre-pardons along with some regular pardons down this way. There are people down here that might just need both." When asked to elaborate, Mr. Gullibilliani just said, "You'll see. You'll see. We need to concentrate on getting the right count. I'm thinking some of those ballots might be disallowed." When it was pointed out that the ballots in the Alleged Woman's trunk had never arrived at the polling station, Mr. Gullibilliani commented, "Exactly. That's just what I'm saying. Why didn't they arrive? Something crooked is going on down here. Just look around."

Bertha "Twelve-Toes" Biggs was standing nearby and edged toward a 50 or 52 gallon barrel. Sheriff Biggs—no known relation—gave her a smile and a nod. Mr. Gullibilliani opened the door to his spider red Mercedes and drove off, however, just as Bertha hefted the barrel and headed toward him.

Breaking News! *Tanks Arrive!* Early Tuesday morning, two or maybe three tanks arrived from the Montgomery installation of the National Guard. The tanks reported to the local Livingston National Guard Armory. "We tore up some highway chunks getting here," one of the tank commanders commented. "Tell the Highway Department we're sorry, but sometimes you just gotta do what you gotta do for the protection of America's property." A helicopter was also sighted, though two or four spectators argued that it was an oversize drone magnified by evaporating morning dew. The commander would not confirm or deny the presence of the helicopter, saying that was "Classified." When asked how many tanks had been dispatched, the commander stated, "Two, I think, though there was something moving behind the one following me. So maybe three. You want numbers, get some Georgia FBI, you want action, get me and the Alabama National Guard."

"Hot damned dang!" Mayor Babette "Babes" Babcock stated, pulling out a kerchief to wipe one of the tank's treads.

Up to the Moment News! *Pick-up Circle Enlarges!* The circle of alleged pick-ups on the Alabama-Mississippi border reportedly has grown. "They've changed from a circle to some type of ovoid. That's their second mistake. Their first was doing this." The local cattle farmer who initially reported the alleged incursion held up three chunks of bark in his hands to show this reporter. "These're from the water oak that has marked the state-line boundary since my great-great-great-great granddaddy's time. And now look what they've done to it. I'm glad they've moved out of that circle formation. It'll open up weaknesses for those tanks and our own pick-ups to take advantage of. I called all three or four of my sons. They're driving their pick-ups over tomorrow and bringing a bunch of friends too. One of the wifeys bakes a mean biscuit."

Mid-Afternoon News! *Proud Bananas Spotted in Bluffport!* Some of you may be wondering when this pretty (and pretty tired!) reporter has time to put on her eye shadow. Well, don't worry, she's got an invisible hand. Ha. Seriously now, the Proud Bananas have been closing in on the Coatopa Fire Station in Sumter County, where somewhere around seven million reportedly COVID-infected ballots are being held for another recount. The Bananas are still threatening to eat all the ballots. "Doesn't matter to us whether they've got that supposed COVID germ or not. We've got hot sauce. They'll be finger-lickin' good. The Kentucky Colonel was a great-great uncle on my momma's side, you know."

Hot and Ready News! *Group Identified!* The one hundred and four or seven alleged pick-up truckers have grown expositorially in number. Concerned local farmers say there are now well over two hundred and ten or eleven pick-ups on the Alabama-Mississippi border. "And some of those fellas have already crossed into Alabama territory. If this was a football game, I guess they would have got themselves a touchdown." Meanwhile, a spokesman for the Mississippi truckers said they have decided to name themselves something patriotic. "M & M's is what we are officially now. Mississippi Marksmen. I guess you know what that means. We're not melt-in-your-mouth candies."

Elsewhere, the Proud Bananas seem to have increased their number also. A contingency of a whole lot of motorcycles joined the group last night. Up to seven or ten teenage girls from the county have been spotted riding shotgun in the pick-ups or on the sissy seats of the motorcycles, waving large American flags. One teenager was yanked off a motorcycle as a wind gust lifted her and the flag and threw both into a creek. The teenager suffered only some cuts and bruises, what the EMT folk know as "incursions, abrasions, and contusions." She and several cyclists spent two hours respectfully drying the flag and searching for a ruby earring the teenager had lost.

News! News! News! *President Requests Talk!* President Trumpet has suggested that the Secretary of Defense for Alabama offer to talk with both the Proud Bananas and Mississippi Marksmen, or the M & M's, as they have come to be called. "They're goo people," the President added. When asked if he meant they were "good" people, the President jutted his jaw out and said, "I am very smart. I always stand behind my talk. Some people have said I should write a dictionary. So they are goo people. Goo people! My supporters know what I mean. Just ask any of them! You people from fake news certainly aren't goo people. I'd say you are just the opposite, "oog" people, in fact, some very oog hombres. When I'm President, I'm going to get the news straightened out." When a reporter pointed out that he *was* President, Mr. Trumpet stated, "That's just the type of disrespectful comment I'd expect from you people. A not goo comment, a very, very not goo comment."

All the News Worthy of Worth! *Alleged Woman Once More Breaks Silence!* "Well, I haven't exactly been one of those holy hermits sitting on a stalagmite," The Alleged Woman commented, "but I do think it's important to note that the Japanese may have stuffed those ballots in that goofy trunk before I even bought that Nissan. When I said that before no one paid attention, I mean not an anyone one ever and no no one, so I'm saying it again, now. Here. Now. The Japanese over in Japan may have stuffed those ballots in my trunk! They may have sent the whole shebang from Japan to America on a freighter. My two darling nieces are going to help me get that factual possibility out. You'll see, you'll see."

Within one or two hours, a spokesman for Nissan Motor Company, Ltd., in Nishi-ku, Yokohama, Japan, said he strongly doubted The Alleged Woman's claims, but that Nissan Motors had requested the VIN from the Sumter County Sheriff's office.

Important Stuff! *Philanthropist Makes Offer!*

Philanthropist Patty "Pearl" Pureheart stated that she will provide napkins, iced tea, and fried chicken if the M & M's, The Proud Bananas, and The Alabama National Guard under the leadership of Alabama's Secretary of Defense will meet at the Interstate rest stop just south of Greene County.

Mayor Babette Babcock replied that there was plenty of farmland in Sumter County where the meeting could be held instead. "We'd like to keep those tanks in the county, just in case," the Mayor stated. "Besides, maybe if national news notices, we could attract some businesses to come here. We've got loads and loads of land and willing workers both. Even a little ol' seed packet factory would help. Long as it wasn't marijuana."

Breaking News! *Unexpected Storm Scatters Ballots!* James "Maybe, Maybe Not" Spann predicted clouds for this entire day. Instead, a thunderstorm swept over the land surrounding Sumter County's Coatopa Fire Station, scattering up to eighteen or twenty Biden Ballots from where they were airing over Highway 28. A reward has been offered for the discovery and return of the ballots, and volunteers from the local high school will soon be combing the area. The CDC has provided all volunteers with purple gloves and pink or black masks. "We need to get those ballots back. They may be infected with the

COVID-19 virus," Atlanta CDC director Doctor Healthman, M. D., stated. "In fact, I'll say it's almost certain they are infected. This is a potential disaster. There's an interstate highway connecting to New Orleans." When asked why the CDC has requested that high school students participate in the search, the Director stated, "We just have to reach out to whatever resources we can. We happened to have those pink and black masks. And the gloves, well, kids just love purple, though you should never wear it on a job interview. I found that out the hard way." When asked for more details about that interview, Doctor Healthman, M. D., replied, "I've got a search to conduct, I don't have time for any more questions."

Instant News on Your Screen! *Dancing TikTok Duo Cause Traffic Jam!* Sumter County, Alabama, is not known for its traffic, but the famous TikTok duo choreographing a search for ballots along Highway 28 backed up logging trucks and travelers for six or nine miles, the congestion reaching out to Highway 80 or 82 that connects Demopolis to Meridian. The Mayor of Meridian indicated this was one more instance of Alabama's incursion on the sovereign State of Mississippi. "I won't say that I support those M & M truckers," Meridian's mayor continued, "But I can say I understand their complaint. And I'd like to point out that no teenage girls have taken up with them, like they have with those Bananas. They're goo people."

When asked if he meant they were good people, the mayor said, "Good enough for America's President, good enough for me and Mississippi. I mean 'goo' enough."

News! News! News! *Date, Time, Place!* Alabama's Secretary of Defense, in conjunction with Mayor Babette "Babes" Babcock, have scheduled a meeting with The Proud Bananas, The M & M's, and the Alabama National Guard for noon tomorrow, that is Wednesday, December 2, on the cattle farm of Louise "Lorrie" Lonely, a lifelong Sumter resident. "This will be just like having FarmersOnly.com show up on my land," Ms. Lonely stated, brusquely brushing brilliant blonde hair from her blue eyes and well-tanned forehead.

Goo News! Goo News! *Ballots Retrieved!* Seventeen of the possibly COVID-infected Biden ballots have been recovered by high school volunteers. After several young couples wandered into bushes and dense covering "just to check out of way places and things, you know," seventeen Biden ballots have been recovered. The high school's principal claimed a moral victory for his students. "In just three hours, our students found almost all of those ballots. We're waiting for the traffic to clear, so that we can get three or four buses out there to pick the students up."

CDC director Dr. Healthman, M.D., warned that two or three ballots were still "wandering in the wind, like vagabond gypsies. We're continuing the search with the manpower we have, though."

The Latest of the Late! *CDC Director Apologizes!* After the National Council of Gypsies excoriated—meaning got very, very mad at—CDC Director Dr. Healthman, M.D., for his recent comments comparing the possibly infected two or three outstanding Biden ballots to "a band of vagabond gypsies," Dr. Healthman apologized, saying, "Some of my very best friends are gypsies."

In other news, philanthropist Patty "Pearl" Pureheart stated that she has contacted the KFC in Meridian, Mississippi, and the KFC in Demopolis, Alabama, and ordered enough Original Recipe fried chicken for tomorrow's confab on Ms. Lonely's cattle farm. "I wanted to make sure that both states received some income. And I just felt that Original Recipe was a more patriotic and peaceful choice. You never know, but all that crispy crunch might incite sore gums and hard feelings. Besides the yummy fried chicken, there will be lots and lots of sweet tea and biscuits." When asked if she ordered Cole slaw or baked or green beans, the philanthropist replied, "We mustn't forget that these are very hungry men, not rabbits."

Aerodynamic News! *A Helicopter Drone!* The Alleged Woman was spotted on her mother's land, along with her two pretty nieces, Jilly and Lilly, testing a third drone. Smoke was spotted coming out of the two airplane drones, while the helicopter tossed off multi-colored sparks. A concerned neighbor extended his garden hoses to the dirt road that the planes were flying over. "No offense, but sometimes you just wish folks would have stayed lying-down-groaning-sick on their damned kitchen floor," the neighbor commented.

When another neighbor questioned whether this drone helicopter was what was spotted days back entering town with the Alabama National Guard, the Captain from the Guard commented that the answer was "Classified."

Some New News of Sorts! *Twins Argue!* "We're not really twins," Lilly said as her sister Jilly tossed her head and walked to the far side of the dirt road, carrying both remote controls for the drones with her. They tossed frowns at one another, and Lilly explained, "We're what's called fraternal twins. Fraternal, not identical, not the always same-same. And that's why I want to tell you I'm sick and tired of everyone saying her name first, 'Jilly and Lilly, Jilly and Lilly, Jilly and Lilly.' It's like a dumb drummer who just knows one beat, *buh-boom, buh-boom, buh-boom.* And, no, I don't care if it is alphabetical order." When her sister Jilly bent down to pick at a weed on the roadside, Lilly cried out, "Sis! Look out! A copperhead!" At her sister's warning scream, Jilly jumped backwards and tripped, falling in the dirt. "See what I mean? Fraternal. I'm smart enough to know it's too darned cold for snakes. Hey wait! Look! It's one of those Biden ballots! Can you believe it? Isn't there a reward? Sis! Kiss and make up! Kiss and make up! Did you keep those purple gloves?"

Breaking News! *Gullibilliani Contacts Governor!* Very early this morning New York lawyer Rudy Gullibilliani visited Alabama's governor, asking her to throw out the seven million Biden ballots and give the state's electoral votes to President Trumpet. Rudy Gullibilliani reportedly joined the governor for buckwheat pancakes with pecans, her favorite morning meal. Later, outside the governor's mansion, he commented, "I understand that some of those ballots are missing now, up to twenty-three of them. Isn't that suspicious? Doesn't that sound crooked to you?" When a spokeswoman for the governor stated that the seven million ballots had never been tallied and entered at the voting station, Rudy Gullibilliani, who had yet to get in his spider red Mercedes turned to comment, "See what I mean? Suspicious, isn't it? Why weren't they entered? I've got to get back to Sumter County. I wouldn't miss that meeting on Ms. Lonely's Two Hot Balls ranch farm for the world."

Clanking News! *Tank Loses Tread! Violence Avoided!* A lead tank from the Montgomery National Guard threw a tread at ten this morning and prevented Alabama's Secretary of Defense from reaching an arranged meeting at Ms. Lonely's Cattle Ranch, known as *Dos Huevos Caliente*. Hence, Ms. Lonely and Ms. Pureheart were left to host the two groups, The Proud Bananas and the M & M's, through lunchtime. The Proud Bananas refused to eat any dark meat from KFC. "White only, bro," their leader proclaimed. "We need to keep ourselves clean and pure and ready." The M & M's, on the other hand, ate every piece of chicken placed before them. Some of that group were even spotted gnawing gristle. A few—the number remained uncertain—peaceable pit bulls circulated, gulping the remaining bones.

Matters did intensify momentarily when some Proud Bananas suggested they might take an alternate route through Mississippi on their return trip after dining on the Biden ballots. "If your Mississippi belles look anything like these sweet Alabama fillies, we'll be happy to detour. We may even saunter." The Bananas were referring to the twelve or thirteen fourteen- to fifteen-year-old girls accompanying them from Eppes, Gainesville, and Sumterville—towns they had passed through in Alabama. Three or five of the M & M's angrily threw down their Wal-Mart Everyday Paper Napkins, bunched their brows, and stood. Two or five pit pulls stood with them. All five or ten snorted.

At that moment, Ms. Lonely, owner of *Dos Huevos Caliente* Cattle Ranch, grabbed a microphone and offered to buy all the participants a six-month subscription to either FarmersOnly.com or Tinder®, their choice. "Just those of age," Ms. Lonely added, as two teenage girls jumped from the lap of a Proud Banana to cheer. Ms. Pureheart, meanwhile, commandeered a pick-up and soon returned with twenty or twenty-four cases of Budweiser.

Breaking News! *Tanks and Guard Delayed!* Joe "JJ" Jo of JJ's Tire Center commented that he couldn't really comment on the ten a.m. call he received this morning other than to say that he had to order a "really special type of tire." When reminded that tanks, if that was to what he was referring, used steel treads, JJ would only say, "All that stuff is highly classified information."

Breaking and Important! (This One's Worth Braking for!) *Last Two Ballots Retrieved!* Fraternal twins ***Lilly*** and Jilly have uncovered the last two missing Biden ballots on an Alabama dirt road. "We thought there was just one, but two of them were stuck together, just like that FBI guy said." / "We don't really expect a reward, we just want our auntie to get her name back. She deserves that." / "Alleged is no kind of name." / "It's not even a goo name." / "Yeah, why can't that President pardon her?" When this reporter pointed out that the Alleged Woman was accused of toting seven million Biden ballots in the trunk of her car, ***Lilly*** of the twins replied, "So? So what's that got to do with anything? We don't really believe seven million ballots could fit in that dinky trunk. Once me and my sister pretend-kidnapped each other. We got all sort of bruises when Fang wanted to jump in and pretend too. There just wasn't any room left. And that was four years ago, when all three of us were smaller. So think about that." / "Yeah, think about that," her sister Jilly added.

Elsewhere, CDC director Herman "Hiccup" Healthman, M.D., stated that all the viral ballots had now been recovered, thanks to the alert eyes of three or four teenagers. "Those girl twins found the last two. And a rolling—I mean roaming—pair of teens from the local high school missed their bus and walked over here with two other ballots somehow stuck to the girl's pink thongs. She said she felt something itching and wondered if it was a tick, but her boyfriend reminded her it was too cold for ticks. The couple requested to be quarantined together until we could administer a COVID test. Their parents haven't been reached, which is why I hadn't let the news about those two ballots out. But now, I think it's okay. Those kids assured us their parents know they're engaged and that she wears pink thongs."

Ms. Patty Pureheart has ascertained that she will provide chicken for the delayed meeting that will take place tomorrow, after a tank threw a tread and delayed the arrival of Alabama's Secretary of Defense.

And Ms. Lonely then announced that FarmersOnly.com had set a one-day record for registrations. "I feel good about that." When asked if she meant "goo," Ms. Lonely only sighed.

Breaking News! *Alleged Woman to Speak!* The Alleged Woman whose trunk was filled with Biden ballots has scheduled a press conference for one hour before tomorrow's meeting on the cattle ranch known as *Dos Huevos Caliente.*

In related matters, a spokesman for Nissan Motors, Ltd. said that the VIN given them by the Sumter County Sheriff's office indicated that the Nissan in question is a 2003 model. "Obviously we couldn't have filled that trunk with those fake ballots. It's against Japanese custom to accuse a lady of falsehood, but she needs to drink some green tea and meditate. Or, not to be mean, but maybe invest in a hari-kari knife and save shame. Nissan Motors is going to ship her a complimentary case of the tea. Meditation is up to her and her spirit guide. Or maybe the knife will work better." The spokesman pulled up his shirt, grimaced, and tightened his stomach. "I'll toss illustrated, step-by-step instructions in with the tea." When the spokesman was told that ***Lilly*** and Jilly, the Alleged Woman's two nieces, claimed to have been playing in the Nissan's trunk four years ago, and that a dog had jumped in with them, the spokesman smiled and tucked his shirttail to comment, "That just shows our Japanese ingenuity. Frankly, and this is off the record, had there been seven million ballots in the trunk along with those two girls and that animal, I would not have been surprised. The trunks are that spacious. And . . . there is a childproof latch on each trunk's inside that will release the trunk when pulled. We put that in because Americans are so prone to kidnapping one another. So those twin girls were safe all that time."

Breaking News! *Meeting Delayed!* Late this evening, Secretary of Defense Jean Highjeans announced that she would have to delay her Friday meeting with The Proud Bananas and the M & M's because of an ingrown toenail operation. When several reporters laughed, the Secretary's face reddened. "Look, I know my humor proceeds me, but this is more like a tumor that bleeds me." When several reporters chuckled, the Secretary straightened and continued, "My doctor warned that if I don't have this removed soon, neither he nor me could be responsible for any decisions I made. The pain is a drain on my brain; in other words, I'd have only birds for words."

Blasting Breaking News! *Afternoon Surprise Witness!* Missy Carvedone, an expert poll volunteer and IT specialist, testified late in Sumter County Courthouse this Thursday, accusing the Sumter poll workers and the Georgia FBI of misplacing up to half a million ballots. "All I can say is, that there may be half a million Trumpet ballots that just disappeared. I don't know what you did with them." Ms. Carvedone went on to explain, "My name is pronounced the American way, 'Carved One,' not 'Car-ve-DON-i' like some whop—no offense, Rudy—way. Say where's the Jim Beam? Rudy, you told me you are a prominent bar member. This is the first bar I've ever been in that doesn't have Jim Beam on the shelf—anyway, there were a lot of Trumpet ballots—maybe up to seven million—that just went missing—I don't know what you folks did with them—maybe some silly business behind that fire engine?—Rudy, come on now, quit tugging on my arm and hand over the Jim Beam—I know you got some in that fancy briefcase of yours." Ms. Carvedone continued for fifteen minutes, until the judge studied the courtroom's vaulted ceiling and called for a recess. "Thank God!" Ms. Carvedone replied. "Let's go look for those ballots and some Jim Beam."

Good Morning News! *Alleged Woman Flies!* The Alleged Woman and her mother and her nieces, ***Lilly*** and Jilly, addressed reporters on Sumter County Dirt Road 17 mid-morning. "I'm not no preacher," the Alleged Woman said, as the crowd of reporters gathered and an early frost evaporated, "so my two nieces and me are going to short and quick show you this message Mom wrote out just after she retired from the post office. It's sort of a tiny poem." The Alleged Woman hugged her mother and turned to her two nieces, "Ready, girls?" At that moment a drone helicopter rose over a nearby pecan tree to hover over the crowd of reporters and a neighbor. When Fang, the Alleged Woman's alleged pit bull barked, a large American flag dropped from underneath the helicopter to float in sunshine, amid a shower of multi-colored sparks. Two drone planes soon appeared, trailing vapor behind them. "We've been practicing," the twin named ***Lilly*** said. "A lot," the twin named Jilly added. They looked up to the sky where the drones had left a vapor trail spelling "*Piece.*" Then the planes flew over again and left another trail, "*Love.*" The sky over the road seemed happy and still to this reporter. ***Lilly*** and Jilly then spoke jointly, "And here's a surprise!" It took a few moments, but soon enough beneath those two words came this phrase, "*Free The Allegid Woman!!!*"

And elsewhere, in a joint announcement Ms. Pureheart and Ms. Lonely requested that the state government provide logistical support for The Proud Bananas and the M & M's who will remain on *Dos Huevos Caliente* Ranch over the weekend. "I'm getting nervous for my cattle," Ms. Lonely said. When Ms. Pureheart giggled, Ms. Lonely said, "Yeah, well that too. Some of those fellas do look kindly desperate around the kidney areas." / "I'm pretty sure all of them are Republican," Ms. Pureheart commented. "It's only Democrats who want to legalize messing around and tipping cows." Ms. Lonely then inserted, "Well either way, we sure could use some help out here."

Secretary of Defense Jean Highjeans quickly replied that the governor was already working on it, and that some top-notch country acts—The Steeldrivers, Dolly Parton, or George Jones—were being contacted for a possible emergency charity performance on Saturday. When a reporter replied that George Jones was dead, the secretary's face fell. "George? Dead? I . . . well Dolly's still alive isn't she? We can only part one great singer at a time. All America has the Jones for country music." When no one laughed, the secretary donned her dark sunglasses and continued, "All the more I'm going to say is that there will be someone out there on Saturday to keep those fellas happy. And guess what? My toe will be all dandy and repaired, so we're going to drive some tanks and things on a piece of land next to that Dos Hoopoos Ranch and do some super loud target practicing, just to make sure those fellas know we mean to protect our citizens and our land."

In news elsewhere at the Sumter Fire Station, not long after Secretary Highjeans' announcement, Supervisor Eve Adams said, "My first cousin, he's president of the local Anti-Fa-La-La chapter, and he says a group of them are going to that farm on Saturday. My beloved fiancé of the FBI tried to talk Cousin Jamal J'Tookie out of going there, but Jamal's got his granddaddy's genes. His granddaddy was just a boy and marched over that Selma bridge. His daddy—well, he's another story. He got shot in a poker game. But Jamal takes after Granddaddy; all the family says so. Sam thinks he can get him on with the FBI maybe. He's that good." When asked if she meant her cousin Jamal or Agent Sam Strong, the supervisor replied, "Both." When asked if she meant to say they were "Goo," Supervisor Adams yelled, "Hell no!"

"Tanks! Hot dang damn!" Mayor Babette "Babes" Babcock commented. "And you know on whose land those tanks are going to be tanking, don't you? And you know who's going to shoot some rounds out of those big gol-durned cannons, don't you?"

In related news, Livingston police chief Billy "Bill" Billingsworth announced that three or four local teenage girls had been reported missing. And Sheriff Biggs of Sumter County said that two or five Sumter County teenage girls were also missing. "And one eighteen-year-old boy drove his pick-up to the county line. It's not even graduation time. He was joined by five or seven others. I hope this isn't some kind of escalation."

Breakfast Breaking Lunch News! *Rudy Gullibilliani Tests Positive!* At three or six minutes after noon today, mostly Central Standard Time, New York lawyer Rudy Gullibilliani tested positive for COVID-19. Speculation has arisen that his handling of the Biden ballots may have been the source of his infection. Directly before being admitted to local Hilltop Hospital in York—not *New* York, just to clarify—Gullibilliani had announced that at precisely 3:42 or 3:46 on election night, every single one of the eight or ten swing states, where President Trumpet had been shown to hold a "very huge and very statistical lead," suddenly flip-flopped in support of Biden. "And all those states were using Dominican Order voting machines. Those machines were installed by the Democratic Party, without any consultation with Republicans. And that Dominican Order company is owned by some foreign entity, maybe in Spain or Venezuela. This is a travesty for American Democracy. Not American Democrats, it's a deep-state coup for them, but for American Democracy." Mr. Gullibilliani coughed several times, but waved away a Kleenex offered by a reporter. It was minutes afterward that Mr. Gullibilliani tested positive for COVID-19. "It's no big deal. I feel fine and I need to stay here to corner the truth on those seven million or even more fake ballots. You just know there were a lot of dead people signing those ballots, maybe even some illegal aliens. You just know a lot of sad voters were turned away by polling officials who claimed, 'I'm so sorry sir, but you have already voted by mail-in ballot.' You know that sad news left some sad voters, some very sad and very confused sad voters, unable to freely cast their vote for Donald Trumpet. So I need to stay here and corner the truth for America. I have the greatest trust in the medical staff at Hilltop Hospital."

Breaking Afternoon News! *Gullibilliani Flown to Bethesda's Walter Reed!* An Air Force One Jet landed in the spacious parking lot of Hilltop hospital at 3:42 or 3:46 this afternoon to transport Mr. Rudy Gullibilliani to Walter Reed Hospital. "Get me out of this yahoo town," a nurse reported Mr. Gullibilliani telling the two attendants who escorted him from Hilltop. "And what's worse, he said that after I'd wiped that drippy brown shoe polish off the side of his head at least nine times," she added.

Soon after, President Trumpet urged Walter Reed to admit Rudy Gullibilliani. "He tried to enlist for Korea, but he was too young. He tried to enlist for Vietnam, but he was too old. He's a very, very patriotic man, the most patriotic man I know. He would have been a soldier if he could have been. And he wouldn't have been captured like some loser."

Breaking News! *Music Group Agrees to Play!* The renowned R & B band Seven Green Apples has agreed to appear tomorrow on *Dos Huevos Caliente* Cattle Ranch and entertain the M & M's and The Proud Bananas. "We're sure looking forward to chomping down on some chittlin's and watermelon and fried okra," the leader of the group stated. "We're going to premier our as yet unreleased single hit, 'Too White for Me Blues.' It's not really a blues piece, more like hot-cake-rap, but we call it blues to get the over-forties crowd's attention. My good friend Jamal told us there was an opening and even arranged the whole gig. We're hyped and hopped and heading to hit hard. And for the record, I was just kidding about the chittlin's. Man, pig intestines! Are you putting me on? Give me some good fried chicken gizzards any day!"

Breaking News! *Up to a Dozen or Fourteen Teens Missing!* Police Chief Bill Billingsworth stated that nearly fifteen or so teenage girls were missing from homes in Livingston. "And the county's numbers are twice that," he added.

"It's not just girls, it's boys, too. And they've taken the family pick-ups," Sheriff Brandon "Big" Biggs commented. "I think it's an escalation."

The Livingston police chief stepped forward to say, "I don't want to be alarmist, but I couldn't agree more."

And in corroboration, at sunset on the western county line of Sumter, farmers reported seeing pick-ups gathering. "They're hanging back on the Alabama side, but their bumpers and hoods are all pointed to Mississippi. It looks downright scary."

Late Night Stuff! *Ms. Carvedone Makes Startling Announcement!* "It's not that I don't believe in getting tested for COVID," Ms. Carvedone stated. "I just don't trust the tests." Ms. Carvedone went on, "You ask me why? Why don't you look at that stainless steel thing that appeared and then disappeared out in Utah for your answer? Why was it there all of a sudden? Why is it gone all of the sudden? Could it be that it appeared when the voting started? Could it be that it disappeared now that the voting is over? Could it be that steel thing was broadcasting messages to all those Dominican Order voting machines across the country? 'Change Trumpet to Biden! Change Trumpet to Biden!' Just imagine what that looks like in binary code! I'm a very smart woman, so I'll just let you guess why that creepy black monument's gone. I'm surprised it took this long. Utah's the perfect place. It's high and it's flat." When a reporter commented that the monolith was found in a canyon, Ms. Carvedone replied, "I've seen those canyons and I've seen those monoliths, and I've seen some awfully crooked looking voting machines made in Venezuela or somewhere. They all needed polishing! I've seen plenty!

Do you have any Jim Beam on you? It's chilly out here. I thought this was the deep South."

Timely News! *Trumpet Declares No-Date Holiday!* In honor of Rudy Gullibilliani's miracle cocktail cure, President Trumpet has declared a No-Date Holiday. "This is something new, something very important and very good that will keep America Great," the President stated in a 28- or 32-minute press announcement. "In honor of one of America's greatest patriots recovering from the Caroming Chinese Curse, I am declaring this a No-Date Holiday. Restaurants and spas and retail outlets will be open. Theaters can open. Churches will be open and free to worship and sing praise and brother-hug in the true American fashion. But no government functions will function. In essence, this will be a non-day day. It will be just like the shifts between Daylight Savings time. I've been told by very smart people that my idea is very smart and will save taxpayers lots and lots of money. So, to be frank and clear, today won't exist for government. No deep-state contractors will be able to bilk the government for today, no mealy-mouthed, limp-wristed state university college professors will be able to preach communist socialism today, no liberal Democrat governors will be able to tell you that you have no freedom today, no librarian will be able to stare at you over their bi-focals today, no PBS announcer will tell you about sick whales today, no namby-pamby social workers will try to politically-correctify you today. Freedom for America! Freedom for Americans! Today will exist just for commerce and just for Americans. Landlords can still collect rent." The President jutted his jaw, to allow more free thoughts to flow. "Let me explain this concept, which I've been told is brilliant, by people who are amazed that I'm not a math scientist. You know how you wake up after a time change and it's the same hour? Well, we'll all wake up tomorrow and it will be the same day. All this to honor Rudy Gullibilliani, and don't forget that honorable Texan Attorney General, Kindred Pixel, whose honorable state is exposing the terrible things that went on in Pennsylvania and three other states. Terrible, terrible things. From my heart, I wish every honest American a happy No-Date Holiday."

Stellar News! *Israeli Astronomer Predicts Joshua-like Phenomenon!* "Aliens exist and they have visited certain people on earth and there's no doubt that they will assist in keeping celestial objects in their proper place during the American No-Date Holiday. President Donald Trumpet is a very smart man, and he is one of a select few who have been in contact with aliens, who, in conjunction with his No-Date Holiday will be slowing, maybe even retro-grading, the sun and moon and planets and stars so that a minor abrasion in the Universal Cosmic Wheel can be corrected." This announcement came from ex-Israeli

Space Security expert Haim Unshed. When asked if the abrasion involved the American electoral college, Dr. Unshed responded, "There's a tear that must be repaired," he continued, "and President Trumpet's No-Date Holiday will assist immensely in this repair. That is all I can tell you for now. The President and I have to take global mental health into consideration and let information flow, but only as popular acceptance will permit."

Elsewhere: Rudy Gullibilliani announced that with the time provided by the No-Date Holiday, he will be able to travel back to Sumter County. In an interview after he received his VIP COVID-19 cocktail and upon being released from Walter Reed Hospital to the cheering physicians, nurses, and staff, Mr. Gullibilliani stuffed a mask in his suit's pocket to announce, "Masks are overrated. They're decorative, like kerchiefs. How often do you need to yank a kerchief from your suit jacket and blow your nose? That's what ties are for. So you can bet I'll be at that ranch on time, now that this No-Date Holiday has come about. President Trumpet is a very smart man. He could be an astronomer and run a calendar company. We won't stop until Americans get what they deserve, the election they deserve, the President they truly elected, without those seven million ballots being stolen from them. I know crooks very well."

And even elsewhere, the TikTok duo led Sumter High School's seniors in a rustic dance alongside Highway 28, since it was a sunny, warm December day in Alabama. "You know, you really can't call it a December day down here," Jesse of the TikTok duo asserted. "That's right," his partner Erin stated. "It's a No-Date Holiday. Watch now, we've come up with a No-Dance Dance!" The duo shook off their tops and twisted and hopped onto some dry weeds to roll together. The entire senior class cheered and followed suit. Within the No-Hour hour, one hundred thousand hits had been recorded on TikTok.

And . . . Rudy Gullibilliani phoned from his loaner Air Force One to comment, "Those kids! The moment I saw them in that high school auditorium, I knew they were going somewhere. Do they have a legal advisor yet? They need to be careful. There are a lot of crooks out there, and well, you know that I know . . ."

And even more elsewhere, Joe "JJ" Jo of JJ's Tire Center reported that he was receiving a record number of calls from Highway 28, where rubber-necking logging truckers and motorists were driving off the pavement into ditches while watching roadside high school couples rolling topless in the sunny weeds.

"Hot damn dang!" Mayor Babette Babcock reportedly shouted as she manipulated a tank's cannon toward a vulture tree. "Every year, those durned things hang out in that tree, looking gloomy and liberal and scary and all. Well, that's going to end here and now. You watch." / "Be careful, Babes, be sure the buzzards are the only thing you buzz," her good friend Jean Highjeans stated. Several crewmembers in the tank reportedly laughed, including Mayor Babcock.

And on a nearby dirt road, ***Lilly*** and Jilly publicly complained they were missing all the fun with their classmates out on Highway 28. "I guess we're a little jealous of the TikTok duo," they said in unison. "BUT," ***Lilly*** iterated with a Sumter County foot stomp, "we're going to do something really important on Saturday." / "If Saturday ever gets here," her sister Jilly added. / "Don't complain, Sis. This No-Date Holiday gives us more time to practice. Doesn't Auntie always say, 'Practice makes Perfect'?" / "Yeah, but look at Auntie," Jilly then added, pressing the control to her drone airplane so that it rolled twice overhead. "Did you see that!? Did you see that!? How's that going to fly in the heartland of Sumter County tomorrow?" / "If tomorrow ever gets here," her twin sister was heard to whisper in an echo.

In a nearby house, The Alleged Woman walked to stand before her bathroom mirror, listening to the drones flying over her mother's rooftop. She tugged at her hunter-red bandana mask, but its GPS alarm shrieked and she could imagine deputies at the sheriff's office racing for their cars and sirens, so she left it alone. The piercing noise, however, brought her two nieces running from the road to check on her. "You'd think," she reportedly told the two, "that on a No-Date Holiday, I could take this damned thing off." / "Auntie!" her nieces shouted. "Potty mouth alarm!" They giggled. "Come on outside. We've got a new trick for tomorrow, or whenever Saturday comes," ***Lilly*** said. "If it ever comes," her sister Jilly added.

Elsewhere, when asked if the FBI still listed the Alleged Woman's alleged mother as a person of interest, Agent Sam Strong commented, "This is a No-Date Holiday. I'm really not free to comment on much of anything concerning the Bureau today. But I can tell you this: Me and Ms. Adams are getting ready to walk down to Highway 28 and join all the topless fun." / "No principal or math teacher to watch over us!" Ms. Adams stated, rolling her ~~breasts~~ shoulders. The two were joined by the Georgia contingent of FBI agents and the volunteers from the Sumter County, Alabama, polling station. Altogether, fifteen or eighteen folks walked down to Alabama Highway 28. Dr. Healthman, M. D., of the Atlanta CDC, stayed behind. "It's not because I don't love clean fun," he stated, "but someone has to be responsible and watch these seven million infected ballots." When reminded that it was a No-Date Holiday and that as a federal employee he wasn't allowed to comment, Dr. Healthman, M. D., commented, "Well then, just scratch that comment. Wherever it itches."

And . . . just as the contingent rounded the bend to

reach said highway and just as this pretty reporter took her right hand and scratched her head, a huge woman hefted a fifty or fifty-two gallon drum, without even a small grunt.

Livingston police chief Bill "Billy" Billingsworth and Sumter County Sheriff Brandon "Big" Biggs reportedly drove their entire staffs to a shooting range to practice. "We're just hoping that crooks will eat sugar cookies and observe the President's No-Date Holiday and that drivers will drink hot cocoa and drive safely to avoid bad accidents. I don't want to be alarmist, but I fear we need to hone our shooting skills for Saturday when everything returns to its rotten Denmark state," Sheriff Biggs commented. Several listeners cocked their heads. One asked, "Isn't Denmark one of those really cold, fishy countries?" No answer was proffered.

And on a nearby farm, from beside a backyard grill, this: "Elvis was a good boy. He loved his momma. I wish I had a boy—or even a daughter—who loved me enough to buy me a Cadillac." The Alleged Woman's mother continued her statement to the press. "Elvis was a good boy and I know that he's squirming his hips around up in heaven. That's why I couldn't dump those stamps. The FBI can arrest me if they want. I gotta stand behind what I believe. And what I stand most behind is that good Tennessee boy's shimmying be-hind! Behind the be-hind! Did you know that that Secretary of Defense and me are fifth cousins? That's where I get my sense of humor. Folks used to visit the post office even if they didn't need stamps, just to hear me crack a joke over the counter at them. They stopped visiting when we installed that COVID Plexiglas. Things just weren't the same, cause it threw my timing. My daughter, I guess she got her sense of humor from her daddy. Which means she don't have a lick of it. Shoot, I'm the one that had to sign for that Nissan of hers. The dealer dropped a thousand off the price just to hear me tell another joke." The Alleged Woman's mother paused. "Oh hell, I shouldn't of said that about her Nissan. It's really hers, not mine. Do you think the FBI will make me wear ankle bracelets or an electronic mask?"

And . . . Dr. Herman Healthman, M.D., of the Atlanta CDC reported, "I know that as a federal employee I'm not supposed to be talking business on this No-Date Holiday, but good Lord in heaven! You should have seen what I just saw! Hoo! That woman should be on WWC Wrestling. She makes Andre the Giant look like Alice the Gimp. She just hefted that barrel and wedged it right in front of that door. Well, that's okay by me. Leaving those COVID-19 infected ballots quarantined inside that fire station is the perfect solution. Hoo! I gotta get her cell phone number somehow. She can come over to Atlanta and straighten a few little matters out. And guess what? She was wearing a mask! A beautiful red-checked COVID-19 mask. Woman of my dreams, where are you, who are you? This isn't politics, this is love!"

Just eleven point three miles north of the fire station, the spokesperson for the Proud Bananas flexed his "Freeedom" tattoo to speak: "Me and the other Bananas are happy for this No-Date Holiday because it allows us to celebrate our freeedoms. We always say we got four freeedoms in America: 'Fucking, Firearms, Firewater, Fried chicken, Fine trucks, and Fifteen-year-old girls." When someone pointed out that came to six freedoms, the spokesman commented, "Yeah, yeah. And here's another freeedom for you: We got the freeedom not to pay attention to wise-head smart-heads who act like the whole world is a math class. No wonder everyone is always wanting a ballot recount."

Camped not far away, the two leaders of the M & M's spoke, on hearing the Proud Bananas cheer: "I suppose those boys are okay enough, if President Trumpet says they are. They're a bit oversexed though. In Mississippi we like to keep sex in prospective." / "That's right," the second leader stated. "We always like to prospect for sex." When someone laughed, the leader continued, "You know, that new Alabama Secretary of Defense thinks she's so funny. Well, we know something about funny too. I heard her and her mayor friend over there shooting off that cannon. Didn't scare me none. I was watching through the scope of my ought-six or seven. That mayor woman missed that tree and those buzzards by a good fifty yards. Not even field goal range." / "But we do need to get serious now," the first leader asserted. "Those Banana Boys need to stay away from our little sisters if they come through Mississippi." / "Roger that," the second leader added.

Elsewhere, on the Mississippi-Alabama border, Alabama-side, up to eighty or a hundred pick-ups had gathered about a bonfire. "We don't got no fancy name, though some of us wanted to call ourselves something like the Nick and Gus and Tubbs Trio. NGTT. But there's too many of us to be a trio, I think. Or maybe not though. I hate math. Hey, you aren't going to give our location out, are you? Some of our dads would be awful pissed. Whoa! Hey! What in hell is that noise? Hey wait, I think it's something I can dance to. It's got a real rhythm." / "I'm hungry," a curly-haired teenager walked up to comment. "I smell fried chicken."

And not far off, another elsewhere, in a garage just one or three miles away: the Seven Green Apples started a final practice session. "Told you, Lady, we don't eat no fried chittlin' pig innards. We got ten buckets of Kentucky Crispy. Those buckets have inspired all of us, so we've ramped up our soon to be released hit, "Too White for Me Blues." We're gonna play it tomorrow. If that ever comes. Who knows what that nut head in the White House is gonna do next? I admit that some of the band are happy about this No-Date Holiday, though. More time to practice. 'Practice makes perfect,' this nice-enough White woman down the road from where I live always says. Her life looks to be a mess to me, though. She should take her own advice. That's what her nieces say too, 'Take your own advice!' We thought about letting the nieces sing in our band, but—" / "But they got no rhythm!" the drummer inserted. / "I was gonna say, 'But they're too busy messing around with little airplanes, dive-bombing my little sis's wild-ass Afro and scaring her."

Dawnbreak News! *Saturday Is Really Real!* President Trumpet announced that Saturday has officially arrived. "This is goo for America, this is goo for freedom. It will keep America Great. Some things have been accomplished, some very goo things, very goo. And I'm going to take this special occasion to tell you that I'm a very goo loser. A very goo one. I understand a lot. People are amazed that I'm not a psychiatrist. So I want now to tell you that if I had really lost that election, I would admit it. I would admit it and I would shake Joe Biden's palsied hand like a goo loser. But I didn't lose it, because it was crooked. Because there were fraudulent votes and voting machines. Widespread. Everywhere, even. But yesterday fixed all that."

And in Israel, ex-Israeli Space Security expert Haim Unshed concurred. "The tear in the Cosmic Wheel has been repaired, I'm happy to say. The entire world can thank President Trumpet. He's a smart man, a very smart man. All that the aliens have asked in return is a Barbie and Ken Doll duo that can do the latest TikTok dance moves and fifty-five or -eight pounds of string licorice. Oh, and a video of the TikTok duo rolling topless in the weeds along some American highway."

Breaking Saturday News! *CDC Director Urges Groups to Social Distance!* This authentic and official 'Saturday' morning, Dr. Herman Healthman, M.D., urged the folks meeting on *Dos Huevos Caliente* Cattle Ranch to practice social distancing. "Didn't they hire George Jones or some country group to sing out there? Singing—flinging off notes and spittle—that makes all the more reason to wear a mask and social distance." When informed that George Jones was dead, the Director commented, "From COVID? When, oh when are people going to take this pandemic seriously?"

And elsewhere, Sheriff Biggs said he expects the Livingston Police to support the county officers at the cattle ranch confab. "We've got pictures of most of those underage girls and we're going to be looking for them there. To avoid confrontations, we've asked the parents to stay away, though some of them are pretty angry and will probably be nosing around looking for their daughters anyway." Livingston's Police chief nodded and stepped forward, "Sad to add, but some of those parents don't care. You might even say that some are happy." Sheriff Biggs pursed his lips and exhaled a slow sigh in agreement. "That's true in the county, too. One mother told me she'd supply whoever took her fourteen-year-old daughter with a year's worth of Sonic Curly Fries and Budweiser."

And elsewhere in the upper spiritual realm, preachers across the nation have urged congregants to tithe twice, since, "The Lord Jesus decreed that Sunday really came twice." This, even though it seemed it was Saturday that came twice. But the Lord does work in mysterious ways as we have all noticed of late.

Mid-Morning Saturday Break! *Alleged Woman Plans Surprise!* Over breakfast pancakes and sausage and tomato gravy, the Alleged Woman has announced that she will have a "pop-up surprise" for those gathered at the *Dos Huevos Caliente* affair. "Me, my mom, Fang, ***Lilly*** and Jilly—we're going to give those boys and whatever girls are with them a treat. You might call it a moral lesson, like a parable or something. This *is* Saturday now isn't it?"

The Stumble That Bumbles! *Ms. Lonely Commended by FarmersOnly.com!* A surprise retinue from

FarmersOnly.com arrived at a little after ten a.m. this authentic Saturday on *Dos Huevos Caliente* Ranch. The retinue reported that they'd stopped outside Memphis for a Hip Shaking and Tobacco Spitting Contest to celebrate the No-Date Holiday. "Did Elvis win? Did you see Elvis?" an elderly woman in the crowd shouted, waving a postal service cap and kicking out a two- or three-step. Five or eight FBI agents immediately surrounded the woman, who held up a booklet of stamps and shouted, "Free Elvis!"

The spokeswoman from FarmersOnly.com asked that the agents release the woman, promising the organization would give her a six-month free trial and would not allow her to post photos of herself in any manner of postal uniform. At a nod from Agent Sam Strong, the five or eight agents complied. A Proud Banana member with enough hair to make six multi-colored wigs stood atop a candy red tri-wheel motorcycle to wave at the woman and exclaim, "Ma'am, ma'am! Over here! I do like spunky older women! Cougar me, baby, cougar me!"

At this, your roving busy, busy reporter could no longer restrain herself. She headed toward the motorcycle, pulling shotgun shells from her bandanna and shouting, "That's my—" But she was cut off by Ms. Lonely and Ms. Pureheart, who both sashayed shamelessly toward the red moronic motorcycle as if they were in a hip-shaking contest, while cooing unprintable and unspeakable coos. *Older, smolder*, this reporter thought while watching their vulgarities, but keeping her thought to herself out of politeness's sake, though a nearby cow did moo loudly, seeming to agree.

Dr. Herman Healthman, M.D., suddenly stepped between the two women and the candy red motorcycle, waving a large placard that read, "Social Distance! Mask up like Poncho Villa!" When four Proud Bananas snarled and headed toward the physician, a very large woman rolled a barrel at them, getting a perfect strike. "Anyone else wanna mess with the Doc?" she shouted. Whoa. Nearly everyone stood seriously studying the ground, which remained where it has always been all these many, many geologic years. The huge woman then waltzed up to Dr. Healthman, M. D., and was heard to whisper through her red mask, "I have a confession to make: I really do have twelve toes." / "I'm a physician. Physical anomalies are nothing new to me," Dr. Healthman, M. D., was heard to reply in a moaning sigh.

Meanwhile, both Ms. Lonely and Ms. Pureheart had pinned The Proud Banana and his hard white banana against his red tricycle motorcycle, which, having those three wheels, stayed stable enough to withstand their ministrations. We surely have Euclid or Pythagoras or some other Greek to thank for this equilibrial fact, your reporter realized.

Bam!

That sound turned this pretty reporter's head, for she thought that Mayor Babcock had perhaps again misfired and hit several head of cattle with a tank shell. But it was the drummer for the Seven Green Apples. The Apples had just taken stage, and their lead singer waved a microphone before his dark face and shouted, "We're proud to be here, with the Marksmen and the Bananas and the Anti-Fa-La-La's, who will arrive at any minute. We're going to open up the show with our first public performance of our soon to be released top hit, 'Too White for Me Blues.' " Before the murmurs could grow too loud, the singer began,

> 'They don't eat no chittlins, and we don't too.
> They chomp fried chicken, they slurp watermelon grooves.
> They're our cousins, must be true, but still I gotta sing,
> Their vibes send out the too white for me blues.
> Yeah, Baby, too white for me, too white for me,
> Too white for me blues!'

The drummer hit some terribly deep thumps on the bass drum, then blasted his cymbal. The lead guitarist ramped his amp with enough high note reverb to hurl Jimi Hendrix to the stratosphere. A coffee-cream woman in golden bangles hopped on the stage and began to booty shake until male eyes bulged, whether they were brown, blue, gray, or green.

'Too white for me, too white for me blues!
When they walk down my street, they looking for
skag.
I don't mind, I sell them a bag.
Their green money spend just like mine do.
But still they vibe out the too white for me
blues.
Too white for me, too white for me!
What we ever gonna do?'

This reporter is witness: it is surely true that music soothes the savage beast, for about sixty or a hundred teenage girls moved from the Proud Banana faction and began bouncing, and the Proud Bananas joined in. Ms. Pureheart and Ms. Lonely got up and shook too, and soon the entire FarmersOnly.com team began stomping and filming from atop their bus, which swayed from their shakes. The M&M's stood motionless for a full minute—well, maybe fifty-four or -six seconds—keeping their arms crossed over their chests. "This ain't junior high school, fellas," the booty-shaking woman shouted from the stage. Oh yes, soon enough their heads began bouncing. Only the cattle remained chewing cud.

"Too white for me, too white for me,
"Too white for me blues!"

Women emerged from the Mississippi pick-ups, tossing half-smoked cigarettes and beer cans to the ground. They began to grind against their chosen M&M.

Even this pretty reporter felt her knees trembling.

The cougar woman with the postal service cap grabbed the Proud Banana away from Ms. Pureheart and Ms. Lonely, leaving them slumped together against his candy red tricycle motorcycle. The cougar spun the Proud Banana about and waved her cap in the air. "Rain, sleet, or snow, Daddy. Let's get it on!"

When Agent Sam Strong started forward, Supervisor Eve Adams grabbed his waist to loudly proclaim, "That woman's a mother. My heart bleeds tulips for her. Let it go, Sam." / "But she's masquerading as a federal employee!" / "Sam, it's Saturday, which is almost as good as a No-Date Holiday. Tell me this ain't gonna be a problem when we're married!"

> "Too white for me, too white for me,
> "Too white for me blues!"

At that moment, loads and loads of restored Buicks, Chevrolet Impalas, and Ford Galaxies pulled into the ranch's front gate, bouncing over the cattle guards. The Anti-Fa-La-La's were arriving. When seventy or ninety Black bucks strutted from their cars, everyone was too busy dancing to notice or care. Soon enough, the Anti-Fa-La-La's joined in the happy motion.

"Say, you're a nigger, aren't you?" a Proud Banana asked as he accidentally twirled his mate into a nearby dancer.

All dancing stopped. Some serious seconds did some serious tick-tocking, as in imminent time bomb, not TikTok, as in frivolity and fun. Tick-tock, tick-tock, tick-tock.

"No," the Anti-Fa-La-La kindly responded. "It's this damned noontime Alabama sun on my skin."

> "Too white for me, too white for me,
> "Too white for me blues!"

At that moment, the barrel that Bertha "Twelve-Toes" Biggs had used to bowl over the four Proud Bananas burst from the lead guitarist's high-note reverb. Seven million Biden ballots floated in a slight breeze.

This reporter gasped. Everyone gasped.

Dr. Healthman, M. D., white-eyed and leaned to shout a warning, but was stopped by Bertha: "Back at the station, I sprayed all them ballots with a mix of bleach and ammonia. Ain't no virus germ gonna live through that." / "Never, never, mix household cleaning supply chemicals!" Dr. Healthman pleaded. "Promise when we're married you'll never, never do that! That mixture you made is in essence the Mustard Gas used during World War I!"

Some Proud Bananas had already started eating the ballots. Some M&Ms were joining in. They all stopped at the word "mustard." They all looked at the ballot in their hand. They all pulled ballot mush from their mouths.

Jamal J'Tookie of the Anti-Fa-La-La's stepped bravely forward. "I got a whole case of Hellmann's Mayonnaise in the trunk of my Buick."

"And we got a couple hundred thousand Dairy Queen hot sauce packets," a Proud Banana added.

The two sped off to fetch. Everyone looked nervously about, studying skin tones until the two returned and spread their condiments on a picnic table.

> "Too white for me, too white for me,
> "Too white for me blues!"

The band resumed playing as everyone chewed ballots now slathered with the condiment of their choice. A calm, munching noise, punctuated now and then by a beer tab's pop, pervaded the ranch. Even the Seven Green Apples joined in the ballot festival, stepping off the stage and pulling a special hot sauce from the drummer's bass. Ms. Lonely's cattle moved closer to the fence line, their big brown eyes watching, watching. Two M & M's walked toward them with a handful of ballots.

"Don't you boys be trying to tip my cows, now!" Ms. Lonely warned.

The sun was rolling happily overhead as cattle joined in the munching. Spurts of chuckles played across the field. The sun rolled some more. Grass weaved; stray ballots were caught up, spiced, and munched. One lanky M & M rubbed shoulders with a short but stocky Anti-Fa-La-La, and the two belted out a pleasant, "Old Man River."

Sheriff Biggs and the Livingston Police chief arrived. They exchanged photographs of teenage girls and pulled binoculars from their cases to inspect the munching crowd. Some ballots flipped by in the breeze, up and over, up and over. The sheriff nabbed one. An M & M, who claimed to be a sixth or seventh cousin to the sheriff, handed him a Dixie cup of mayonnaise.

At that moment, Mayor Babette "Babes" Babcock and Alabama's Secretary of Defense Jean Highjeans bumped an entourage of personnel carriers and tanks over the cattle guards of the ranch. "The music stopped and it got too quiet. We were worried," Mayor Babcock explained, giving a cautious wave from atop a tank. She and the Alabama Secretary of Defense nodded to the police chief and county sheriff. The chief and the sheriff covered their mouths and stopped chewing, like two kids caught with licorice jellybeans.

"What Babes means, you know, is that old adage I've always heard: 'When the hopping stops, pull out your Glocks,' " Alabama's Secretary of Defense pronounced from the lead tank's turret. Three guardsmen riding on the tank laughed, elbowing one another. "Told ya she was a joker," one of them commented.

From the crowd came a burp, which started a chain reaction of burps and belly rubs.

There were maybe only four or ten thousand ballots left. After a nod from the Secretary of Defense, the entire Alabama National Guard debarked and started eating the ballots, adding the drummer's special hot sauce. "You should bottle and sell this stuff," the guard's captain commented with a smile. "You could call it 'Too Hot for Me Sauce!' "

The drummer gave a laugh and said, "Say, you're Black, ain't you?"

"Man, thank you, thank you, thank you. These folks have all stayed too constipated to notice."

"So, do you got the Too White for Me Blues?"

"Just like you got the Too Hot for Me Sauce. You

know, these ballots don't taste half bad."

"That's cause they're for Biden, even if they never made it there."

Your pretty reporter's attention was drawn from this conversation as five guardsmen gave a grunt and tipped the bowling ball barrel to spill out the last of the ballots. Fewer than a hundred ballots fluttered to the ground. A guardsman knelt to tug out three or five more.

At that moment a spider red Mercedes slid up. Both doors were flung open. "Guard those ballots!" A man and woman shouted this simultaneously, running from the Mercedes. It was Rudy Gullibilliani and Missy Carvedone, and they both frantically dove for the ballots, coming up with two fistfuls each. The pair ran to the bus and gazed up to its roof, from where the crew of FarmersOnly.com stood filming.

"I want you to get all this on record," Mr. Gullibilliani shouted, "because it's important for America, land of freedom." He waved his fists with the ballots, and Ms. Carvedone followed suit. "This is interference with federal evidence, this is witness tampering, this is abominable." / "He's exactly right," Ms. Missy Carvedone yelled. "They might as well throw these ballots in the river for catfish to purr against!" / "This is just what I'd expect from the Biden camp," Mr. Gullibilliani inserted. "I know crooks very well, and this is just what I'd expect!" Mr.

Gullibilliani shook his left fist of ballots. One dropped and Missy Carvedone dove for it, dropping several herself as she did, but then kicking out with her stiletto heels to spear them.

"This is just what I'd expect from some devil-may-care, cow-loving, Democratic blue county! How many of these ballots are signed by dead people, I wonder. Three, four, even eight times. You know, I could subpoena them all, call them all forth as witnesses. Make them swear on a Bible, a goo Bible, not some liberal version that allows cattle-love. And then just what would they have to say? They'd be caught with their brittle fingernails packed with grave dirt and black ink and sad lies. 'Fifteen times? Twenty? Is that how many votes you cast while you were dead? Admit it. Go on and admit it! Here's the proof right here! Right here before you!' Then I'd shake the ballots before their sunken grave-filmy eyes and make them see! 'Can you deny that this is your signature now? On thirty ballots! Have you no shame?' "

"Rudy, you'd hate to have to do that to dead and deceased folk, wouldn't you? Make them appear in court and all?" Missy Carvedone asked, pulling four ballots loose from her stiletto heel and standing.

"Justice calls for harsh measures! I want to ask those of you filming and recording this from up there on that bus's roof to note that I have a thousand—a full thousand with three or more zeros—that many witnesses, just as solid and honest and reputable as Ms. Carvedone right here before you. Witnesses from a lot of states. A lot of very goo witnesses from a lot of states. I could name those states. I could name those witnesses. I could. In less than four minutes. And each of those witnesses has seen voter fraud. Some have seen just one instance, some have personally seen up to fifty thousand instances, maybe even a hundred or two hundred thousand. Some, like Ms. Carvedone here, have worked with or inspected the fraudulent Dominican Order voting machines. Where were those machines made, anyway? China? Venezuela? Did Hunter Biden personally insert little nibs in each one? Or more to the point, did his daddy Joe Biden insert those nibs and collect a thousand dollars each time his foul fingers fibrillated? Is that how he purchased those two purebred German Shepherds on a vice-president's salary? But let's put economics aside for a moment. I want to stop right now and ask all of you gathered here just one tiny question: Can you look me in the eye and tell me you doubt that ten thousand or even fifty thousand votes in Arizona were cast illegally? Arizona? Are you kidding me? Are you putting me on? Are you trying the old Brooklyn dead-end street gang pounce on me? The entire sandy state of Arizona is overrun with illegal aliens who are all voting, voting, voting! In Arizona, they don't even need dead people! They've got illegal aliens!"

"Aliens!? Rudy, I thought you told me that only President Trumpet and that Jew guy could see the aliens!"

This reporter watched Mr. Gullibilliani reach for Ms. Carvedone's arm; she watched Ms. Carvedone screech and shake his hand loose.

"Let me speak, Rudy! Where is justice now? When you told me about those aliens, I told you that I thought they were taking over that stainless steel deal in Utah and maybe using mind rays to make people vote for Biden. It's bad enough those machines all used binary code to change votes for Trumpet into votes for Biden. Magic? No, fraud! Fraud, fraud, fraud! But those aliens weren't satisfied with fraud! No, they had to take over minds! Get your hands off my arm, Rudy! Let me speak! Freedom! Where's the beer, where the liquor you promised? Where's the justice?"

At that moment, a blonde-headed, blue-eyed Proud Banana popped a beer and handed it to Ms. Carvedone. "A gentleman, at last," she commented.

"One thousand! One thousand goo witnesses!" Mr. Gullibilliani yelled as Ms. Carvedone slammed down her beer and looked about for another. "I can promise you that this isn't over yet. Those fake electors can all vote however they want on Monday, they can cast their votes for Biden if they don't want to vote for their conscience, if they want to act like zombie-fied robots. They know the election was stolen. Stolen like a Brooklyn hubcap! I know crooks very well. They all know. We all know! Everybody knows!"

"I told you, Rudy. Their brains. The aliens."

Lilly and Jilly evidently were listening from behind a small shed. They started to move out, but The Alleged Woman shook her head at them, so the two girls went back to eating ballots with mayonnaise.

Mr. Gullibilliani held his ballots tightly and grabbed Ms. Carvedone, who was also holding her ballots tightly and craning her head. After the same blonde Proud Banana handed her a second beer, they got into the spider red Mercedes and drove off.

"Hey! Alabama has an open container law!" one of the sheriff's deputies shouted, swallowing the last bite of his ballot and the drummer's hot sauce.

The Seven Green Apples took to the stage again.

> "Too white for me, too white for me!
> Too white for me, too white for me blues!"

Tired and Bedraggled Sunday News! *Very Early Morning, Late Night, Not So Blue Blues.* The Seven Green Apples played until 1 a.m., when the drummer announced that he had to get to church in the morning.

When hissing and catcalls mounted, the drummer explained, "I gots to meet my girl there. She sings in the choir. I love her more than chicken gizzards and gravy." A contingent of women from the M & M's cooed at that. Their cooing and the sound of popping beer tabs replaced hisses and boos.

Bertha "Twelve-Toes" Biggs hoisted Dr. Healthman, M. D., on her shoulders to announce, "Herman played drums in a band in high school. If you folks don't mind a White man, he can beat out a beat or two. He's got blues in his soul. He's got a lot of blues in his soul. All twelve of my toes can promise you that."

And so the band played one-and-a-half more hours, until the piles of bodies resembled the ballots in the trunk of the Alleged Woman's car, all snug and slumbering.

Sunrise Sunday News! *A Pronouncement, a Minor Miracle.* If you've ever watched whirly seeds whirl down from a whirly seed tree, then you'll know what this day was like. The sun came up chilly, but happy, like a sun should come up.

On either arm, in her armpits really, but don't worry, The Alleged Woman always gives a double swipe to her deodorant, this reporter found the twins ***Lilly*** and Jilly snoozing. That's correct. That was no binary code typo from Utah flipping out over your Internet. That was no fake news. The Alleged Woman is I, me. This restless, pretty reporter is me, I. We are one and the same. Me and I, I and me. It is what it is, I am what I am. The Alleged Woman comes clean.

So I guess I may as well give it to you straight from here on, straight up the middle, like Mom always says.

The Alleged Woman's mother, my mother, always gets up with the sun, no matter the time zone. This Sunday sunrise, she brushed the Alleged Woman's nose, my nose, with her postal service cap. Then she brushed her granddaughters' noses—***Lilly***'s and Jilly's noses—with that same worn cap.

"Mom, COVID-19!"

"Don't you worry none. I had Randy here tested by that doctor last night. He's negative, though I have to tell you, he's got one great big huge and hot dangling positive—"

"Mom!" This reporter covered both ***Lilly***'s and Jilly's ears as well as she could with only two hands.

The Proudest Banana, ol' young Randy of the candy red motorized tricycle, was suddenly standing behind Mom. He held a tray with three cups on it, two hot chocolates and one coffee with lots of cream and Stevia, just like I like it.

Mom dangled some Elvis stamp booklets in front of us. I've never taken the Hoover Number Assessment Protocol course, but there were surely close to fifty-four booklets. When one of the twins—I'm not going to stir jealousy and say which one—began slurping her hot chocolate too loudly, Mom raised her finger to her lips. "Sh, you'll wake all the nice people and the cows out there. We've got to be nice to the cows, because they're creatures with feelings and brains smarter than a lot of others, and we've got anoint the people on the forehead, just like those Catholics do, except it won't be no Roman voodoo we're using, it'll be straight Memphis Baptism fighting off some other Italian stuff."

"You mean Mr. Gullibilliani," the twins spoke in unison.

I'm always so proud of them. My sister did such a goo job. I mean such a good job. It is catching, you know, this sad disease, whatever it is. I want to say it's stupidity, but it's more than that. Or less. Or different. Or the same. Whatever, it seems a good deal more viral than COVID-19.

"You need not worry, dearest ladies," Randy said to the four of us. "I believe that beer-guzzling woman and that New York fellow have departed for far, far away, perhaps off to a galaxy many light years hence," Randy said.

"No sir," I assured the young, grammatical, Wookiee-looking lad. "He and his boss and Ms. Carvedone won't ever go away. Not ever. They'll be here for Christmas, for New Year's, for Inauguration Day, for every day you can imagine."

"For Halloween?" Jilly asked.

"Especially for Halloween."

"Come on, children. Drink up. We have work to do. That sun's moving along." Mom tugged a few more Elvis stamp booklets from her apron—Mom always wears an apron—and began divvying them up. "Eight for you, Eight for you, Eight for you . . ."

"Where did you learn to count so fast, Ms. Alleged Woman's Mom?" ***Lilly*** asked.

"I was a poll volunteer. I always counted in multiples to confuse the Republicans watching. I bet I doubled up and sneaked by at least 70 thousand ballots on them that way. Every election year."

"Really, Ms. Alleged Woman's Mom?" Jilly asked.

"You might need some more hot chocolate," I said. "You aren't awake yet, if you believe that whopper. And stop calling her that silly name. She's your grandmother."

Like a magical elf, Randy produced another tray with two hot chocolates and one coffee.

"You girls, when you finish your hot chocolate, I

want you to start over by the fence and that sleeping brown cow. Paste an Elvis stamp on everyone's head. And when you do it, you should whisper this, 'We have eaten the ballots and they are us.' That's important. Whisper it so you don't wake anyone. But it's important. I've got a bad feeling about this afternoon coming up, so we're going to need a little Elvis spirit help. Elvis has some powerful mojo still left in those hips of his. Randy and me will start at the other end of the fence. Daughter, you go straight up the middle. That's what you're good at. Now, what are we all going to whisper when we stick Elvis on?"

"We have eaten the ballots and they are us," we all replied.

"Hey wait!" ***Lilly*** said, even as Mom smiled her wisdom tooth smile. "Where'd you get all these Elvis stamps, Ms. Alleged Woman's Mom? The FBI said there were only eleven booklets."

"And Ms. Adams said there were only ten. Either way, how are we going to Elvis stamp all these people out there, Ms. Alleged Woman's Mom?"

I didn't even bother to remind them she was their grandmother. Don't ever tell teenagers not to do something. That's the moral here. They'll always do just the opposite. "How many fish did Jesus have?" I asked the twins instead—I admit in a bit of a snit, but also saving my mom—their grand mom—the trouble. Mom loves parables and fairy tales almost as much as I do. The twins looked at me like I was some kind of math or history teacher, as if I should have known better than to reach beyond TikTok and YouTube.

"That's easy," Randy replied. "Two. And five loaves of bread. Um, I think that maybe it was, um, uh, Wonder Bread?"

When no one laughed I asked, "You don't happen to be related to the new Alabama Secretary of Defense do you?"

Breaking News! *Huevos Means Eggs! Boys Beware!* After "anointing" nearly everyone on the ranch and even a couple of cows who had eyed us with especial jealousy, we turned to Ms. Lonely's front porch.

"Damn! That's where Rudolph is. Double damn," Randy exclaimed.

"Potty mouth!" the twins screamed, shaking their fingers and giggling. As if they don't blab out more before their second period English class is through.

"I don't understand, though," Randy went on. "How did it get up there? I've got Rudolph's key right here in my pocket."

I felt tulips for Randy's confusion. Then I underwent

a vague vision of Bertha "Twelve-Toes" Biggs hoisting up that motorcycle after everyone else had gone to sleep, maybe at the request of Ms. Lonely, or maybe Ms. Pureheart. Or maybe both. When she hefted that bike, Bertha had given off a huge grunt and a wheeze. "It's a lot heavier than I figured!" She then belched a twelve-toed belch, which scared some of the cattle. I remembered her stumbling three steps clearly enough in the moonlight, one stumble for each wheel, a quarter for each toe? Math. Remind me to tell you what happened in the seventh or eighth grade about math.

Anyway, the motorized, candy red tricycle was now up on that porch, and those two women were cuddled in one another's arms across it, lying obvious post-kiss, post-coitus, post-whatever you can think up, bra straps showing—one black and one pink—hair bedraggled, lipstick smeared. A couple of scratches here and there. Tough love?

"Girls," Mom said. "Look the other way."

"Oh Mom, give it up. Three of their best friends are lesbian."

But I shyly admitted my own surprise until Mom reminded me of an afternoon at the local Piggly-Wiggly. "You had just gotten your journalism degree from the local college," Mom reminded me. "I was going to buy you some champagne, providing that you wouldn't drink it with that redhead boy you were screwing."

"Ma! The twins!"

"I thought you told me they'd heard all this and more."

"We don't have to hear it about our favorite auntie, Ms. Alleged Woman's Mom," ***Lilly*** said.

"But you do need to go on with the Piggly-Wiggly story," Jilly added.

"Those two—" Mom indicated the two women asleep atop the candy red three-wheeler— "were fighting like cats over the last pack of cheese-filled wieners. And guess what your most favorite auntie did?"

"She led them out to the parking lot to her Nissan and opened the trunk, which was filled with seven million cheesy wieners," both twins said. They can be awfully chirrupy and annoying at times.

"No." I held up a finger. "I remember now. I pulled two Ziploc bags from my purse and told Ms. Lonely and Ms. Pureheart they could split the pack and the cost."

"And the moral?" my mother asked.

I had to think a minute. People were waking up, coughing, belching, yawning, and passing gas—all the things humans share with cows to murk the ionosphere into a zerosphere. "The moral must involve something about true love and wieners," I said lamely, to the amusement of Randy. I sure hoped Mom moved in with him, instead of vice-versa.

"Not just any wiener, Daughter, but cheese-filled wieners. But you're right: it does involve true love. Anyone willing to share a pack of cheese-filled wieners with another anyone is heading hard down the road to Forever Fairyland Love." Mom looked at Randy. "Would you do that for me?" / "I sure would," Randy said. / "Puke," one twin commented. / "Aww," the other one said. I think the eldest by five or nine minutes said the latter, showing that her hormones were taking hold. Or maybe it was the eldest that said the former, showing that her common sense was taking hold. I don't know.

We gave the honor of Elvis-stamping the lovers atop the tricycle motorcycle to the twins.

"Just don't get any ideas," Randy huffed, looking askance at the two sleeping, cuddly, embracing women and their bra straps.

"For God's sake, Randy, they're sisters." I wanted to put another stamp on his forehead and airmail him back to Michigan.

"I meant about sleeping on Rudolph."

"Get your mind out of the gutter, Daughter. You're going to need to use it in just a little bit from now, I've got a hard, bad feeling."

"You keep saying, that, Mom. What do you think is going to happen that already hasn't happened? Is everyone going to toss all the ballots like cookies so that we have to recount them for the eightieth time?"

"Seventy-ninth," the twins said.

See what I mean about their being chirrupy and annoying?

Breaking News! *The Fake Truth Revealed!*

"Daughter, I've got to tell you something about those ballots."

Oh ho, now we all were leaning and listening. Randy stopped wiping off his motorcycle where Ms. Lonely and Ms. Pureheart had slept on it—they having awoken to stand in wobbly-legged love—we've all stood on that unsteady pavement, yes? Those two stopped wobbling and looked at Mom. I tugged my red bandanna and looked at Mom. Even the twins, who were heading to fetch the two Ms.'s one coffee and one Earl Grey tea, stopped in their tracks to look at Mom.

"You. I should have known." I narrowed my eyes over the damned bandanna. "Five weeks before Election Day. The gas mileage on my car dropped by a half.

That's when you dumped them in there, isn't it? I even bet they're what wore my back tires down—"

"Don't be worrying about trifles. I'll reimburse you from my postal pension. But those ballots were fake."

"Of course they were fake!"

"No, I mean they were fake-fake. Faker than the fakest news you ever watched, faker than a televangelist's tears, faker than some high school boy's back seat puppy-love groans and whines—girls, are you two listening? Faker than all that. Those ballots originally had Donald Trumpet's name on them."

"Seven million of them? You mean that Donald Trumpet and Joe Biden were actually in a dead heat?"

"Of course not. They were fake-fake. Remember your uncle Joe Smithers from up in Winston County?"

"The one who's in the Klan?"

"The one and the same, that's him."

"That's *he*," Randy said. *Please, please motivate that candy red trike back to Michigan.*

"Well," Mom continued after giving Randy a pinch, "your uncle and a bunch of Klan boys got to worrying that maybe the Blacks were going to steal the election, put in Mr. Biden instead of Mr. Trumpet. Put in Doug Jones instead of that Auburn football coach. So they printed off seven million ballots and filled them in."

"I bet someone had to show them where to put the X," I commented. I'd met some of Uncle Smithers' Klansmen buddies and they surely weren't the brightest sheets in the laundry . . . though they surely were the whitest. Oh my . . . I hope I'm not related somewhere way back to Jean Highjeans.

"You aren't far from wrong about that, Daughter. It's the truth. Your uncle, my brother, admitted the same. Told me he had to point out the right circle at least ten thousand times, said his finger got sore and his eyes crossed. He'd drove down from Winston County all drunked up, that's why he told me all this. That, and he wanted to know if I still had any pull with the post office, could maybe get those seven million ballots mailed in for free. Well, you know how he is with liquor. He passed out on the ratty brown couch that Fang sleeps on. I called up cousin Bertha and she come over and lifted those ballots from his pick-up and put them in your Nissan's trunk, but only after we'd changed the vote on all of them to Biden."

"You did all that while Uncle Joe was passed out?"

"We had to pass him out eight times. Bertha kept plying him with Old Forester Bourbon—his favorite—and then we'd go back to changing the names. The twins helped, got some of their classmates to help, too. I made them all double-dog swear to secrecy. We didn't have time to change the senate vote, though. I'm not in favor of having an ex-Auburn coach making decisions for our state, I have to admit."

"Football, puke." That came from the twins. I sorta had to agree with them. I gave them a nod toward the shed and they left to let the adults hash things out. While Mom was talking, I could hear the buzzing engines of the drones coming from the shed.

"So anyway, we got all seven million ballots changed and fed your uncle some red-eye gravy and biscuits and sent him on his way. Still so liquored that he didn't even notice the ballots were missing from the bed of his pick-up."

"What are you telling me, Mom? That you and Bertha Biggs are the reason I'm wearing this electronic mask?"

"Oh no, Daughter. It's a lot more complicated than that. It's an anomaly, just like Bertha's twelve toes."

An earth-rattling shout broke up Mom's tale.

Broken News! *The Spider Red Mercedes Makes Dust!* Bertha "Twelve-Toes" Biggs stands over seven feet—and that's without her high heels, which she certainly favors when she has a steady boyfriend. To be sure though, those heels are never open-toed. Poor Bertha, like all of us, she endures a crippling complex about some minor deformity. Hers can be covered with tennis shoes or boots or closed-toe high heels. Some politicians have a deeper deformity that would require a roll of Duct tape around their mouths and maybe another around their dicks. Some Q Anon conspiracy theorists have a deeper, deeper deformity that would require a lobotomy. Frontal, parietal, occipital, *and* temporal.

It was one in need of the former, accompanied by one in need of the latter, that cousin Bertha spotted in the spider red Mercedes coming over the hill leading to *Dos Huevos Caliente* Ranch. "That hotshot red car's coming back!" Bertha's shout rattled windows, it scared off birds, it caused an overhead cloud to scud off—was too chilly for mosquitoes or it would have scared them off, too. In short, anyone who wasn't awake before, was now. And on waking, they blinked like everyone else had, and giggled—male or female—at the Elvis stamp stuck on everyone's forehead. They then placed a hand and felt, like everyone else had, their own forehead and giggled some more.

The cattle began to moo. They were hungry. Ms. Lonely and Ms. Pureheart walked off to open the gate to the field of winter rye grass.

Just a bit before, with sunrise, the contingent from FarmersOnly.com had been joined by the Meridian and the Tuscaloosa TV stations and their news vans. Camera crews had cheerfully brushed elbows in a COVID 19 greeting, then hoisted themselves and their morning coffees atop their respective vans to start filming.

Mr. Gullibilliani and Ms. Carvedone headed directly to those vans. They still held two fistfuls of ballots each. Maybe they had clutched them under their chins all night, while we were out here dancing. My mother turned to me and gave a Cheshire cat grin. With her pointer finger, she touched the Elvis stamp on my forehead and whispered, "We have eaten the ballots and they are us." Yeah, I guess I had eaten a ballot late last night when an especially handsome M & M pulled down my mask and put one to my lips, telling me how good it tasted with that 'dusky drummer's sauce.' I figured that 'dusky' was pretty polite, all things considered, so I ate the ballot with the sauce. It wasn't bad, I have to admit. It didn't hurt that the M & M was tall and his blue eyes quivered.

Now Mom gave me a wink as Rudy Gullibilliani and that woman began addressing the cameras, shaking the ballots in their fists.

For the ninety-seventh or the ninety-ninth time—who can keep count?—Gullibilliani repeated the same line. His number of witnesses had grown modestly—all things considered—to fifteen hundred. The number of voting irregularities had zoomed, however. Four witnesses from a state he "could identify saw ninety-two, ninety-three, ninety-four, and ninety-six thousand irregularities." Ms. Carvedone swayed perilously and said the Democrats had kept her from getting eighty-nine different jobs. "I'm very good at IT, very good. That's why I know those Dominican Order voting machines were receiving binary directives from that stainless steel monolith in California—" / "Utah," one cameraman from atop the FarmersOnly.com bus shouted. / "There was one in California too!" Ms. Carvedone retorted.

I'd heard just about enough. People were scratching their behinds and yawning. I could see Ms. Lonely's cattle eating winter rye and swishing their tails in a nearby field. Ms. Lonely and Ms. Pureheart were returning from that field, arm in arm. Doctor Healthman, M.D., and Bertha were playing footsie under a picnic table. I figured she had an unfair advantage. Mom and Randy were polishing his bike. *Please ride it back to Michigan with him, Ma.* Agent Strong was rotating his head in time with one cow's swishing tail, while Supervisor Adams looked admiringly on. Yes, it was nigh-on time. I coughed loudly and the twins peeped from behind the shed. I gave a nod and pulled the transmitter for the helicopter drone from my pocket. I saw their shoulders rise in anticipation. I heard the three drone motors winding up. Showtime!

Lilly, of course, had to prissy off and have her drone make a corkscrew in the air before any vapor trail appeared.

LOVE

The two drone planes spelled out in vapor, while the helicopter popped Fourth of July sparks below. For a moment, everyone looked stunned. It didn't take the FarmersOnly.com crew long to focus on that love word, though. Was like a free advertisement.

BROTHERHOOD

That word came next. Rudy Gullibilliani's upper lip gave off a snarl, though I'm certain he would have called it a "Brooklyn Smile."

PIECE

This was the next word. I had tried to correct the twins quite several many times—eighteen or fifty!—as to the spelling. Mom thought it was the school system's fault. I wondered if the twins and their three lesbian friends and the TikTok duo weren't having some sexual innuendo joke. Maybe the Alabama Secretary of State's personality was spreading. It was happening with Trumpet, so why not with her?

FREE THE ALLEGED WOMAN!

This was the last one. I still had to wear that blessed electronic mask. I was tiring of it. I wanted to get out and boogaloo. And by that word I mean dance and cavort and party, not blow folks into bloody corpses.

Breaking News! *Drones Mistaken for Alien Saucers!* While I was staring wistfully at that last vapor message in the sky, Missy Carvedone shouted shrill enough to give Bertha Biggs competition:

"ALIENS! It's the ALIENS!"

Folk scrambled to their pick-ups, their motorcycles, their personnel carriers, their squad cars. The field filled with weapons, some legal, some illegal, some military grade, some fifth grade. I set my helicopter control on the ground, but the twins kept flying their drones.

Shots, shots, and ever more shots were fired upward. *Can't perch on a stalagmite like a hermit forever, gal. You gotta join something,* a voice rang in my head. I ran to my pick-up, tugging at the mask, where I'd taken to storing a couple of .410 shells, just to keep my cheeks warm. I loaded my shotgun and fired into the air.

The shots kept on. Hundreds of them. Thousands.

Sort of like Gullibilliani's witnesses, I guess. I heard the two tanks fire their cannons and machine guns, felt their recoils in my legs. A personnel carrier was equipped with a flame-thrower that spewed into the air. Mayor Babcock was surely firing one of the cannons, so I worried about Ms. Lonely's cattle, but none was hit. In fact, nothing was hit, not the drones, not the helicopter, not a tree limb in the area. It was like all the bullets, pellets, and projectiles were interfering with one another, ricocheting into each other to cause mayhem, but not grief.

Mom rolled on the ground, cackling wildly, her legs peddling like a four-year-old's. She tugged at Randy's pants while he fired his pistol into the air, stopping to reload three times. It was a mad-minute deluxe. A mad ten minutes, truth be known. And my mother never stopped cackling, even when the twins set down their controls and unpacked the .22's their Uncle Joe Smithers had given them for their sixteenth birthdays, to begin firing into the sky.

Breaking News! *The Miracle of the Loaves, Updated.* Please remember as you read the following that I am a trained journalist, not some wide-eyed poet or science fiction writer.

Holiday sparks from the helicopter became erratic. It then began to Elvis-shake and rattle, until caramel-coated popcorn drifted downward in great, warm abundance. Slowly, folks shifted from shooting to grabbing at the popcorn. Above the helicopter, the two drones once more spelled out something in the sky. I wide-eyed at the shotgun in my hands, the twins wide-eyed at the rifles in their hands. The three of us searched for the controls on the ground. When caramel-coated popcorn stuck in the twins' hair, they began to laugh and catch the falling kernels. As for me, caramel popcorn is pretty close to my idea of hell tugging at my teeth. We all looked to the sky:

P E A C E   O N   E A R T H

"It's the Dominican Order machines!" Missy Carvedone screamed. "They've taken control of everything!"

The only sound after her shout was my mother, still cackling, even louder now, on the ground. My eyes narrowed. *What's that in your hand, Mom? In your hands, I mean. Could it be two little black box drone controls? And one in Big Bertha's plenteous, agile toes also? Et tu, Bertha?*

Now they both were cackling. Cackling, cackling, cackling, until Randy joined in. My shoulder was sore from the shotgun, but what the hey, I joined in. The twins stopped munching caramel corn to join in. Dr. Healthman joined in. Agent Strong and Eve Adams holstered their .45's and joined in. The sheriff and police chief joined in. Mayor Babcock and Jean Highjeans jumped from the turret and joined in. Soon everyone was cackling and eating caramel popcorn: the M & M's, the Proud Bananas, the Anti-Fa-La-La's. Even the cattle out in the winter rye started to romp and kick.

Only two people weren't cackling: Rudy Gullibilliani and Missy Carvedone.

"I'll be back," Mr. Gullibilliani shouted, stomping off like The Terminator even as people cackled. "It's not over until it's over."

Randy ran up and handed Missy Carvedone a beer, giving her a bow. She gave a little curtsy in return before getting into the spider red Mercedes. When Randy trotted back, Mom stood to give him a hug. "Good job," she said. "Did you remember?"

"We have eaten the ballots and they are us," Randy replied, pushing out his chest.

Oh hell, maybe he'll be okay living here. I can move out to the guesthouse and take the grill with me.

Soon to Be Breaking News! *New Year's! Inauguration Day! Easter! Independence Day!* My prediction is for a cold, harsh, turbulent, and morbid COVID winter; a warm, sickly, bed-ridden, and uncertain inoculation spring with lots of hidden eggs, some gooey chocolate, some gooey rotten; and finally a hot, bumpy, but recovering summer.

First thing after the *Dos Huevos Caliente* affair, the sheriff agreed that since there was no more ballot evidence within the state and his jurisdiction, I could toss the bandanna mask. I've grown used to it, though, and I swear I can still smell the Red Man chewing tobacco from where that tall M & M tugged it down. I contacted a preacher who preaches at the Methodist Church in Livingston. He's one of the few preachers I can stand to hear, though my heart still lies with Emily Dickinson and I still prefer to have a wren for my chorister. But Reverend James LaFriend is going to perform a triple wedding on Inauguration Day come January. The Strong clan, the Adams clan, the Healthman clan, the Biggs clan (with all their toes), the Pureheart clan, and the Lonely clan (restoring a revived, original meaning to *Dos Huevos Caliente* Ranch)—they all will be represented. Who knows, maybe that tall, blue-eyed M & M who's been coming to our local bar and buying me beers will show. Oh ladies, I do believe in equality, so I buy him a round now and then too, since I have my job at the newspaper back. Four weddings then? But I have the twins to think of, so maybe I'll hold off until Independence Day for goo example. (Ho. More and more, I suspect that Jean Highjeans and I are related. I'll have to ask Mom.)

Oh, and Mom says not to worry about Missy Carvedone: Randy dropped an Elvis stamp in her beer. Missy's a true believer; Mom and I expect she'll move on to Elvis appearances by Inauguration Day.

Gullibilliani and his jut-chinned pal, though . . . well, you know what they say about bad pennies always showing up. And those two already have a replacement for Missy: the football coach turned senator, Tommy T. Tubbs, who claims he's going to challenge the electoral college vote and cause some real mayhem. Hopefully, no grief will accompany it. Ah, if only T.T.T. would go to announcing college football, if only his two mentors would pair up for a reality TV show. Or even better, if only we could put ankle monitors on the lot and release them in a distant field of rye grass . . .

Happy New Year! Happy Inauguration Day! Happy Easter! Happy Independence Day! Happy Labor Day! They had better be happy. Who could put up with another year like 2020? The twins warned that I'd better stop with Labor Day, that I'd better not mention Halloween, the way this year is going.

"But you just *did* mention it," Lilly says. Or was it Jilly? I look over my right shoulder for luck and see them both standing there, reading everything as I type it out on my computer screen.

"Adults, you can't tell them anything," Jilly snips.

"They'll always do just the opposite. That's why this country is in such a state."

"That's why we watch TikTok," Lilly adds, in her smarty-pants mode.

"I just hope you girls aren't right," I tell them.

"For once, we do too," they respond, getting in the last word, like the coming generation should.

Will the real Fang please sit?

Joe Taylor has published several novels and story collections. Like Alabama's Secretary of Defense, Jean "Jennie" Highjeans, he has long been known for his rollicking sense of humor. He lives in Coatopa, Alabama, which lies just outside Livingston, Alabama, which is close to Meridian, Mississippi. In sum, in the exact middle of nowhere. There he and his wondrous wife Tricia and their twelve dogs and two cats abide pleasantly. The photo above was taken by Tricia, and it depicts the true Fang.